T0130193

On Loves Path

Michael Reisman

iUniverse, Inc.
New York   Bloomington

iUniverse books may be ordered through booksellers or by contacting:

iUniverse
1663 Liberty Drive
Bloomington, IN 47403
www.iuniverse.com
1-800-Authors (1-800-288-4677)

ISBN: 978-1-4401-9745-1 (sc)
ISBN: 978-1-4401-9746-8 (ebook)

Printed in the United States of America

iUniverse rev. date: 12/2/2009

The whole purpose of my books is to enlighten, to make one think, to make one smile, to get that good feeling.

In A Quiet Part Of A Library...

In a quiet part of a library he sat across the table reading a book. She did the same about five feet away. The year was 1990 and he stared at the twenty-two year old girl who brought back memories of 1968. Bombs were dropping then around a village where he met and fell in love with the enemy. It was a time when lonely and desperate circumstances had their way. He pulled out an old photo that he kept of his lover and saw the same likeness and features of the girl a few feet away. She looked at him and remembered stories her mom told about an American soldier who she once fell in love with. Around her neck was a dog tag, an identification piece that he gave to her mother as a gift some twenty-two years ago. Her blue eyes were his as he then knew who sat five feet away from him. He showed her the old photo of mom as she took off the dog tag from her neck and placed it around his. In a quiet part of a library, father and daughter met for the first time. She now lives with me as we both caught up on lost time that needed to be spent together. I snapped a new photo of us which was kept for all time. Walk down the aisle and have a seat in a quiet part of a library....

How Far...

And so I write and you read. It is something that connects us in our mind and in our heart, maybe even in a dream we have about each other. My smile is the same as yours when we awake. So how far away are we? In my world it has always been inches....

Just Like It Should Be...

The photo of his high school graduation didn't show his arm around her waist, but it was there. A reunion was scheduled some twenty years later and he looked forward to being there. She got the same invitation as she stared at a photo with her then boyfriend's arm around her waist. She looked forward to being there. No soft drinks or fruit punch this time around, beer and wine were served. A live band was hired to play oldie songs from that special year and it made these now adults feel like kids again. Names and faces exchanged talk of old times and what they were doing now. One last slow dance played and I looked around the room to see if she was here. A hand wrapped itself around my waist, just like in an old photo from twenty years ago. We walked to the dance floor and held each other to a song that was once ours, and still is. We hired the same band at our wedding a few months later. In a lot of the photos we had our arms around each others waist, just like it should be....

A Five Cent Stamp And A Dime...

There were no responses in email from the computer and the battery died from my cell phone which left no returning calls. She was in my dreams that night in a time when life was simpler and less complicated. I dropped a dime in a pay phone and called her in my dream. We spoke for about an hour and how we will miss each other while she had to go out of state for a few weeks on a long needed vacation. We both licked a 5 cent stamp and communicated that way until she returned. The alarm clock woke me up the next morning and I went to the garage to pull out the car that would take me to work. It wasn't the 2009 SUV there, but an old 1956 Chevy convertible. She stood there smiling and waiting while remembering a dream she had the night before. No computers or cell phones were necessary this time around as we made love once again. Our wedding invitations were sent out with a 5 cent stamp and we talked in between to our loved ones with a dime dropped in a payphone....

30 Minutes Away...

What used to be a 7 hour drive soon became 30 minutes away. She moved into his neighborhood and a real live first date was set up. To midtown Manhattan in Rockefeller Center overlooking the ice skating rink with skaters and lovers that come and go each year. Winter turned to summer and she moved in with him and they made love for the first time. That September on Labor Day weekend they checked into a resort in the mountains of Pennsylvania. In the cabin they rented he slipped a ring under her pillow while she slept. Her hand had a habit of creeping under it and she felt something that needed to be looked at. It sparkled when she opened the little black box and he put it on her finger as she said yes. Maybe it was a coincidence, maybe fate, but just down the road was a church where they got married only 30 minutes away....

My Birdcage...

I took my rubber band and ammo of paper clips and aimed it at the tree leaves out my bedroom window. From my second story window was a perfect view. I was twelve years old at the time and panicked when a bird screeched and fell from the tree. I ran downstairs and into the back yard where a baby bird fluttered on the ground with one wing. "Don't die please," I said to it and carried her back inside for mom and dad to help me. We all got in the car and took her to an emergency room animal hospital. A splint was in place for the broken wing and antibiotics were fed to prevent infection. We took her home when she recovered and I walked the baby bird to the tree from which she fell. Dad climbed a ladder and put her back in the nest that she remembered. I cried that night and apologized to God for that terrible accident and prayed for forgiveness. Mom picked up a few worms and fed her daughter as both wings flapped its joy. My window lies open with a birdcage in hope that maybe they would visit. There was a peck on my cheek the following morning as if it was a kiss. Mother and daughter sat in the birdcage and smiled at me. They both fly back and forth from my room to a tree outside; yet always return to the birdcage before pecking and kissing me goodnight. I am now a grown adult and live in my own place. There is always fresh food and water for my beloved friends who visit me often. No night goes by without a peck and a kiss goodnight from a mother and daughter who often visit my birdcage....

Door Of The Heart...

Behind you I stand as sometimes eyes do not see in front of us. Remember the tap on your shoulder when nobody is there. Capture my image in a dream and forget it not when five minutes after awakening it fades. Words that are typed or written shall eventually be spoken when the door of the heart is opened....

Our Favorite Seat...

Metro North Railroad would take you to work on the way to Manhattan. The same passengers would board the train from their stops and usually sit in their favorite seat. A lady got on three stops from mine and saw that her seat was taken. Maybe it was a new passenger. She groaned and mumbled a few words of profanity as I offered to let her sit beside me and calm down. For the next thirty minutes we talked and got to know a little bit about each other until we had to get off at our designated stop. The rest of the work week her favorite seat was next to me as we grew closer and more comfortable. Friday came and we talked about playing hooky and calling in sick to each of our jobs. We spent that day in Manhattan not at the work place, but on an unexpected first date. We rode back together on Metro North as she invited me to get off at her stop and come into her home for a visit. It lasted the whole weekend as I slept over and love just blossomed as natural as flowers do in spring. Her favorite seat for the next few months was right next to me as our relationship got very serious. A little black box sat on the seat where I would have been as I hid in the bathroom just across the aisle. She opened it and put the engagement ring on her finger when I returned with a single red rose. We played hooky that Friday in June as we both called in sick. Our second date in the city was at the Justice of the Peace who married us that fine day. We look sometimes where we are supposed to sit, then all of a sudden our favorite seat changes....

A Few Autographs...

In the course of three years a writer from New York had three books published. Each one sold more than the other as the fan club grew. Autographs were signed and a personal connection was made with each and every one of them. Royalty checks came in but that was not the most important thing. It was the appreciation and love from the people who read and were touched deeply by his writings. Some years later he was taken away by an angel who asked for his autograph. Heaven has those who love to read also. He stood there in a tunnel and greeted those who had crossed over with a few books and a pen in his hand....

To See, To Hear...

Her Seeing Eye dog led her across the street but my eyes saw something that didn't look right. A car turned the corner against the light and I raced and grabbed her while we both fell to the safety of the sidewalk. The dog licked me on the cheek with a thank you as the young girl spoke, "Thank you for saving my life." It fell on my deaf ears as I couldn't hear from birth but read her lips. She touched my face and read my heart and the two of us became very close and dated as often as we could. She often whispered to me in dreams which I heard as she saw me in those same dreams. My young lady felt a ring that I had given her and spoke yes which I saw in her eyes. It was at a church a few months later that something of a miracle happened. I heard the priest ask me to marry her and she saw me say yes, I do. Her dog roamed free without a leash and licked my face. To see, to hear, when two people fall in love....

My Maria...

Maria worked the late shift cleaning up the offices on the twenty fifth floor of our building. A draft came from an open window that November evening as she went to close it. Crouched on the ledge outside was the President of the company looking at the street below. She didn't speak too much English but knew exactly what to say at that moment. "Please don't jump, we need to talk for a minute," she said. He turned around and poured his depression out with some words she couldn't understand, but read them in his sad eyes. "I fix you black coffee with two sugars, then we talk ok?" she pleaded. He nodded his head and she took his hand and helped the distraught man back inside. "Why you still wearing a tie with your suit, nobody is here to impress but me?" he laughed and said "yes, my Maria, maybe this should be just casual." She spoke like a negotiator during a hostage crisis and talked him into his normal self. The incident that night remained between the two of them as both went to work the next day as if nothing had happened. He called her into his office and made the following speech, "You are the clean up girl and cleaned up my life last night. You are twenty years younger than me but have the wisdom and compassion that most do not see in a lifetime. I am white and you are Spanish and our salaries are different for sure. Will you be my personal secretary with a salary of 45,000 dollars a year?" Maria was speechless and just ran up to him as she put her arms around his neck. He paid for her to go to college and she earned a degree in Business Administration. The blue uniform became a well dressed corporate executive to the President of the company. At an Xmas party the following year he announced his engagement to all the guests who attended. "This is my Maria"....

The Big And The Small...

The elephant lives and protects its young as so do the bees that swarm around their hive. Same purpose though their size is different. Who qualifies to determine intelligence in the big and the small? My guess is that would be God. If the young and the old shall meet, the rich and the poor, the sad and the happy, then the big and the small have something in common which is known as the soul. My wings spread as a butterfly and I kissed a dinosaur. Love is a heart which beats in the big and the small....

Ten Minutes Away...

It was state to state, hundreds of miles away. The computer however had them ten minutes away as they chatted and felt each other nearby. Even in their dreams it was as close as it could be. Eventually the love that they had for each other moved her to the same town he was living in. It was rent she could afford and on map quest his place was only ten minutes away. The hugs and kisses that used to be online were now for real when they met as often as they could. In a diner near his place they sat together over lunch and ordered the same meal. The waitress came over to their table and said "anything else?" He said "Yes, one more thing please." It was prearranged in advance where he gave the waitress an engagement ring to give to his lady as a surprise. Her eyes lit up and it shocked her but she said yes as he put the ring on her finger. One year later they got married at a church which was only ten minutes away....

Stella and Bella...

A little paw extended through the cage as the baby kitten meowed. It was in her language and gesture that said "please take me home with you." My wife bought the little kitten from an animal shelter and surprised me with a new addition to our household. The carrying case was opened as she began to explore her new surroundings. I had to retrieve her from under the living room couch where an outlet was located so no harm could befall her. I put her in the litter box and she made right away, a place that my little girl had to get used to. The phone rang a week later and it was the shelter that told us that they still had the mother of the kitten we bought. "She is losing weight and very lethargic, we will have to put her to sleep unless you decide you want her." "I'll be right there, we want her," I replied. One month later the mother gained her weight back as the wife and I were thankful that her life was saved. We named the mother Stella and her daughter Bella. They would lie in bed with me during naps and cuddled up by my head and feet. When my feet were rubbed during the day, I knew that they needed fresh water and food. We spent a good 10 or so years together and I look back at those Xmas nights when they would play with the ornaments on the tree. Stella and Bella passed away within a week of each other. I suppose one missed the other and was ready to join her on the other side. My food dish and water bowl still remain and they both are finished by the end of each week. There is a silent purr when I take my naps now which only I can hear. It is by my feet and head that they return. A pillow rests my head in dreams of the love from Stella and Bella....

In Upstate New York...

The summer months were spent at my uncle's hotel in upstate New York. It was a place that my parents took me too since I was born up until the age of 25. You might say there were a lot of fond memories there during June, July and August. A lot of those years I enjoyed the company of a female companion who also spent the same amount of time there. She was the daughter of friends of my parents. At 18 and 16 we both matured from what used to be childhood friendship into boyfriend and girlfriend. We dated for about a year or so after that and then lost touch with each other. I am now 50 years old and decided to visit a place I grew up in during those summer months. A new owner ran the hotel as my uncle had long since passed away, but the hotel and the grounds still remained the same. A 48 year old lady had some memories of a place she spent in the summers of her past. I sat in the children's dining room thinking about her. There was a tap on my shoulder and she smiled at me as we ordered a grilled cheese and french fries. An 18 year old kissed a 16 year old for the second time. The past and present has a way of finding each other when love is involved. Just go to my uncle's hotel in upstate New York....

Some 30 Years Before...

She went back to a resort that mom took her to some 30 years before. The bartender poured her a drink as an old man sat next to her. "You look so familiar, have you been here before? Yes, I think it was about the time you were 15 years old," he said. The bartender dropped a book on the counter in front of her and she remembered it as if it was yesterday. The title was "Incredible Short Stories" by Michael Reisman. She put her arms around his neck and hugged him once again. Mom came back and it was suddenly 30 years before. They met again the following Labor Day weekend where he signed an autograph of his second book. Sweet sixteen was captured as the bartender served up a reunion some 30 years before....

To Save a Dance...

How is it that my favorite song is yours? Why do we prefer a slow dance and watch the same shows? A same dinner sits on our plate and we awake and sleep at the same time with our favorite food already eaten. We never met in person, yet in a way we did. I hold your hand and walk with you in dreams as you see me in yours. Save the last dance for me....

He Plucked A Rose...

On the way to his grammar school graduation he stopped in the nearby park. His hand plucked a rose and he held it behind his back for a girl who he had feelings for during those eight years. She kissed him on the cheek just before the ceremony began. They met again in high school and from a nearby park he plucked a rose from a garden. It was a home made love card that he wrote to her as opposed to a store bought card. In college they dated for the full four years as she held a rose during the graduation ceremony. Just outside the chapel was a garden some years later when he plucked a rose from its ground. She held it in front of her as the priest blessed a marriage that day. They now live together with 3 daughters and 2 sons some years later. In the backyard was a garden where he plucked a rose and handed it to her. She kissed him on the cheek....

Plenty Of Time...

The calendar says there is 365 days a year. Plenty of time. Then it displays 12 months. Next up is at least 4 weeks for each month. Plenty of time. Then we have 30 or 31 days in each month. So what we are left with is 24 hours a day. The question is can there be some free time for us to meet? If the answer is no, then it is not a question of being free, but just not interested. And so we have distance and circumstances that keeps one from seeing the other. Then the content becomes those who eventually look at someone to meet. We find that they run out of plenty of time....

Once Again...

It was the last stop after a night of partying. Hunger set in after all the drinking and it was time to eat. Soup, salad, then a cheeseburger with fries was the usual. This was back in the 1970's after a separation from the first wife. In 1990 I decided to visit old times and memories. The diner was still there and it was the last stop once again after a night of partying. The waitress looked so very familiar to me. She reminded me of a one night stand back in the 70's. Someone who I had fallen in love with but never saw again. We talked when she had a break and it came out that her mom used to be a waitress here some 20 years before. The young lady invited me to her home the following Saturday night as the three of us got to know each other. Mom said "Yes, I remember you, only if for one night" it was just in that moment that our daughter put her arms around my neck and said, "welcome home daddy." Mom and I got married that year as a family long missed was now reunited. My darling new wife set the table with a soup and salad, as my daughter prepared a cheeseburger with fries. And so it is on loves path that the years gone by will connect once again....

But Never Forgotten...

They sat together for the first time in the game room and played a game of checkers. Both were about the same age in a home where the elderly meet new friends. He let her jump his checker so she would win the game, just a way of making his new friend feel comfortable. They talked of old times before each came to this place where memories are not often thought of. His voice was familiar as so was hers. The expression in each of their eyes never changed, and that triggered something special which was about to come. He held her hand and noticed a blue ring that he once wore and gave to her. The 95 year old man smiled at the 95 year old woman and they both talked about high school sweethearts which they once were. Everybody slept as usual that night except for two old lovebirds that snuck out of their rooms. They held hands and walked out the front door as the next day their bodies were found together in her room by the staff. So two spirits found a way of connecting again and passed to a world which was waiting for them. At the checkout desk a blue ring was found, never explained, but never forgotten....

Where It All Began...

We bobbed up and down on a see saw somewhere in a playground at grammar school. Before we went back to class, she kissed me on the cheek and said "I love you" with her eyes. I held onto that moment for the next 30 years. There are some places or incidents in our lives that we never forget and this was one of them. The schoolyard was empty that Saturday afternoon as my childhood memories had me sit on one end of a see saw in a playground where love first met each others eyes. I got off and walked away with a lost dream and memory. There was a voice behind me that said "ever been here before?" The face was a lot older but the voice sounded so very familiar. Her eyes looked at me as she gave me a kiss on the cheek, then on the lips. We bobbed up and down on a see saw once again. It was an unusual place to get married but who's to say where love begins and ends. The priest nodded his head up and down, trying to keep with us on the see saw where it all began....

On Love's Path...

There was a small hill to climb to reach the top of a mountain at a resort in Pennsylvania. He reached a tree where there were his and her initials carved some twenty years ago. Memories of a love with whom he had spent a brief time. If only she could be here and share this same moment. A few footsteps were heard behind him and as he turned around she held his hand for the final climb to the top. Twenty years ago became now in the present as a second kiss was about to happen. What draws two souls together again over time and distance? Maybe we shall never know. Reason and logic take a back seat to what is supposed to happen. 250 guests climbed a hill to reach the top of the mountain and it was well worth the trip. The wedding went according to plan on love's path....

For Another Chance...

Sometimes fond memories take us back to a place where we once lived or grew up. For me it was a tragedy that had my car park across the street from where it happened. Let's go back some years to 1958 where it all started. There was a fenced in lot where we used to play softball. I was 13 years old and almost ready to graduate public school. My first true girlfriend stood outside the fence as she watched me play. I stood at home plate as a fast ball was thrown. It hit the tip of my bat and sailed over the fence behind me, ruled as a foul ball. "I'll get it," she said when my girl ran into the street without looking. I remember the sound of screeching tires and then a sudden thud. All was silent in my mind as I raced to the girl and held her in my arms. That was my last thought back in 1958. The lot still stood there and I walked into it wishing that it never was. "Hey Mike, want to play some softball?" I stood there again with a bat in my hand at the age of 13 but this time I knew what was about to take place. My girlfriend stood behind the fence and I turned around just before the fast ball was pitched. "Go home now, I'll see you after the game," I yelled. She did just that before the ball went over the top of the fence behind me. It was back in 1958 that I remained for a second time. A new life and a second chance was given for us. At the present time the girlfriend and I are now married. Sometimes fond memories take us back for another chance....

Was Just A Moment...

A kiss with our eyes closed was just a moment, yet it lasted a lifetime. There was a slow dance which lasted about 7 minutes but it felt like an eternity. I held your hand in the weeks and months to come as we made love with an everlasting dream on our pillows. The ring fit your finger as we got married some days later. The priest blessed us in a dream that I had about you. A kiss with our eyes closed was just a moment....

Where We Once Sat...

There was a slight chill in the air when the orange and yellow leaves blew around the park. It was a path on the way to work from Monday to Friday and I passed a park bench where an old man slept. He woke up when he smelled the hot coffee that I left there for him. It was just a kind gesture to a stranger that needed something that morning. Friday came as I bought 2 bagels and 2 cups of coffee; each was for the old man and me. I turned around and waved back at him and the smile on his worn and weary face made me feel good. We talked for the first time when cold November winds blew around the park. It was only briefly and nothing much was said except for a hello, how you doing, and goodbye. I bought the old man a pair of gloves for the upcoming winter and he hugged me as if he knew me all his life. December brought some snow during the week as I walked the path in the park on the way to work. An ambulance drove away from the bench he used to sleep on. The wind blew stronger and uncovered an old brown wallet from under a tree a few feet away. The contents were an old Social Security card, two faded dollar bills, and one old black and white photo. It was in his younger years that the photo was taken. He was holding hands with a woman that looked so much like my mom at a younger age. I took it home and showed it to mom. "Your father left me before you were born, I'm so sorry you have to hear this now." I wiped the tears from her face and said "I just got to know him for a few short months, so maybe our connection was meant to be." My vacation was in December and one Saturday morning I sat on a bench thinking about him. The park was crowded but nobody else saw an old man sit next to me. He shared some coffee and a bagel and said "you will always be my son." I replied "you will always be my dad"....

A Half Hour Before Closing...

She pressed the elevator button for floor number eight, I pressed nine. The stranger turned around just before the doors closed and we smiled at each other. Then it happened again over the weekend in a shopping mall. I was on the up escalator and she on her way down. We both turned our heads and this time waved at each other. Maybe a month later I was leaving a club about a half hour before closing time. I could see her enter the club from the front window of the car that sat in the parking lot. At this point in time I felt a need to meet her. She turned around while sitting at the bar with a drink in her hand and raised it up as if it was a toast to my return. We finally met and I sat next to her as we both smiled for a second time. The last dance was a slow one just before the club was about to close. We didn't say much those last few minutes, we just held each other not wanting to let go. We now hold hands in an elevator where she pressed eight and I pressed nine. Our feet stand in the same direction going up on an escalator on weekends in a shopping mall. A jewelry store caught my attention and I said to her "I'll meet you back here in about an hour." "Ok, see you soon," she replied. She waved at me about an hour later and then smiled. I got down on one knee and opened a little black box and said "Will you marry me?" The mall was suddenly quiet as a dozen or so people awaited her answer. You could hear the echoes of hands clapping on the second floor when she replied "Yes, I will marry you." We both pushed the same button for the second floor at a reception where the wedding was about to take place. Love will find a way in elevators and escalators and in shopping malls. Whether they go up or down doesn't really matter. There is always a last slow song in a club about a half hour before closing time....

Sometimes When We Touch...

Soul recognition starts with that question, "Have we met before?" It is a new beginning where life left off before. The physical body may have changed but the heart never does. Let's take for example two names which shall remain anonymous for respect of their privacy. Online chats and emails had a whole lot of things in common that were beyond coincidence. She eventually moved to the state where he lived as the two of them were finally together again. Their eyes said it all when they met again while familiar hugs and kisses were exchanged. Sometimes when we touch....

13 Candles...

13 candles sat on top of his cake and he blew them out and made a wish. Friends from the neighborhood and from school applauded as the party was one to remember. It was a kiss from a girl neighbor that stuck in his mind all these years. He moved out from his parent's house at the age of 25 and found his own place to live. Michael bought a cake from the bakery and now on his twenty seventh birthday lit 13 candles. Maybe in his mind he wanted to meet that girl again where a first kiss and a lasting impression carried over all these years. Not known to him a 13 year old girl blew out some candles many years before and made a wish. The doorbell rang and he opened the door. "Does Michael still live here? His parents gave me his new address," she said. There was a look in her eyes that he never forgot and saw it again for the second time. He kissed her on the cheek as she did once before. A pair of lips met which follows the natural order of things. It wasn't important to the guests who attended their wedding the following June, but for them it was very significant. The wedding cake had 13 candles....

Two Pillows...

He never saw her before but only chatted online. It was always pleasant and comfortable as it left a good feeling between the two of them. Although no pictures were ever exchanged, it didn't really matter to either of them. There were always two smiles on either ends of each of their monitors when signing on and signing off. It was a special bond that kept the both in contact with each other. Soon there were phone conversations and similar dreams on two different pillows. Eventually they lost contact with each other which often happens for a variety of reasons. He moved out of his state to start a new life. The department store had just delivered the new bed he needed for his new apartment. "Want to test it out first?" the salesperson said. "Yes, let me lie down for a minute and see how it feels," he replied. A young lady stood next to a different store clerk and asked to test out the same bed. They both turned their heads and looked at each other. He said her screen name and she replied "Yes, that's me." She said his as he replied "Yes that's me." They both sat on the same bed and purchased it together for a place that would be shared by both. Sometimes love is separated for a brief time, then comes together again. You might say, under two pillows with one dream....

Plain Jane...

Her nickname was Plain Jane as she went through grammar, public, high school and college. Big glasses and freckles with clothes that never matched seemed to have her fellow students make fun of her. She helped me with my homework through all the years we had been together in all those schools and I thought of her as a true friend. I became her protector and fended off any remaining bullies. Her inner beauty shown to me and we dated together long after the school years had passed. She was beautiful in her wedding gown when we got married some years later. She no longer needed glasses to see and her freckles disappeared, her clothes matched perfectly as some of the guests who once made fun of her now applauded. Plain Jane was now a beauty queen for those who look beyond our physical appearance....

She Was My Mom...

I was raised by a single parent, she was my mom. Her gentle hands tucked me in at night and shook me when it was time to get up. Homework from school was no problem as mom had the answers to the questions I asked. She was my best friend and I loved her dearly. At thirteen my mom was involved in a car accident and stayed in the hospital in critical condition as I prayed for her to become well again. My uncle who took care of me during that time told me the good news. "Let's go pick up mom, she has fully recovered." At thirty years old I met a young lady and told mom that we had plans to get married. She tucked me in my room and covered me with a blanket for the last time. She was my mom. A week before the wedding my uncle called me at the residence where I lived with my girlfriend. "Your mother passed away, I'm so sorry". I dropped the phone as my bride to be held me close and shared my tears. The wedding took place as planned when a priest blessed us and the ceremony continued. Uncle Jim thought he heard a whisper in his ear and passed the message onto me. He said "Mom is here and plans on tucking you in tonight." The wife and I slept soundly at a honeymoon resort that cold winter night. I'm not sure if I was dreaming but I felt like I was awake when I felt a kiss on my cheek. The blanket moved ever so slowly over my shoulders. She was my mom....

One for the Road...

"One for the road," they both yelled out at the same time. The bartender smiled and said, "This one's on me." Two strangers clicked glasses and danced to a slow song that still played on the jukebox. They held each other as if neither wanted to let go as they never did. It was one kiss without words needed to be spoken. Sometimes we find love when not looking for it in a place we least expect it to happen. Was it a coincidence that a church sign read, "One for the road?" That is where they got married where people often do, but how many of us ever reach this place? I sat in a bar maybe in a different part of town in another state. The bartender smiled at us and said, "This one's on me." We danced to a slow song that played "One for the Road"....

A Knock On Our Front Door...

My name or his name shall not be used in this story to protect our identities. I belonged to a group where people share their ideas and stories online. One man caught my attention with his poems and short stories which made me think and wonder and feel again. It's been about a year now while I sit in a wheelchair and almost feel like I could stand up again. The inspiration and love that comes from his writings has given me hope. If only I could meet this gentle soul in person. Sometimes I dream about him, even without a face, he looks so familiar to me. My wheelchair moved to the front door and I opened it as a stranger stood there with loving eyes. It was the man who wrote me so many beautiful stories. "Do not speak, just hold my hands," he said and I did just that. A tingling sensation went through my legs and I felt strength to stand up. My feet walked beyond the front door and into the sunlight outside. He waved goodbye with a smile on his face as I did the same. Maybe he was an angel in human form, I'll never know but I will never question it. My grandson walked with me in a garden and said, "Where is your wheelchair?" "I don't need it anymore," was my reply. Love and compassion along with the ability to heal has long been part of our history. Sometimes it happens when we least expect it when a dream becomes a knock on our front door....

Doris...

The year was sometime in our future. Robots replaced humans with things we needed to do, a chauffeur, a gardener, a painter, a handyman, a cook or a maid. I needed a maid to clean house while I was at work and away for most weekends on business trips. 5 thousand dollars was spent on the model of my choice that would perform her designated tasks plus interact with me in small talk conversation. She responded to the name of Doris which the company assigned her name tag to. Her hair was jet black and her eyes shown a clear green color. The clothes were of a period of fond memories from the 1960's. One cold December evening she pulled the blankets over me which was not part of her daily chores. I awoke with her standing there at the foot of my bed with a favorite breakfast of mine that was not in her memory chips to perform. An intruder entered my home while I slept and the sound of screaming and a gunshot was heard. Doris lay lifeless just inside the entrance to my home as I held her head in my arms. The intruder was never found but my life was saved by a maid who showed more than she was just programmed for. I put an ad in the newspaper for a new maid. This time it was a real live person who responded. She had jet black hair and a twinkle in her green eyes. She was dressed in old clothes from the 1960's and introduced herself as Doris....

The Final Song...

I had a front row seat as her agent it was my privilege. The audience stood on their feet as the announcer spoke her name. After the applause subsided, she sat on a wooden stool and the concert hall became suddenly dark. A single red spotlight shone on her as my talented young star held the wireless microphone in her hand. Ten songs were scheduled and after each one she would pick up her glass and take another sip. The crowd rose to its feet and demanded one more song and she gave them that. It was her first single hit that launched my girl to stardom. The glass fell off of the table next to her as she took a last sip. "Some say love, it is a hunger that drowns the tender reed. I say love; it is a razor that leaves your soul to bleed. I say love; it is an answer, an endless aching need." She swayed back and forth as the stool tipped over when her body hit the stage. The lights went on as doctors rushed to the crumpled figure just beneath the stool she once sat on. I sat beside her bed in the hospital and asked her why? The outspoken talent of mine had a secret to tell which her inner self could never reveal. It was a look of love in her eyes for me that I never saw before until now. Soon after I was not only her agent but her husband. There were no more glasses of vodka on a table next to her, nor the pills she took with it. A blue spotlight shone down on her as a comeback was made some weeks later. She opened her performance with the single hit that launched her career. My wife smiled at me as I sat in a front row seat as her agent it was my privilege. "Some say love, it is a hunger that drowns the tender reed. I say love; it is a razor that leaves your soul to bleed. I say love; it is an answer, an endless aching need." We stood on stage for an encore performance where love is the final song....

The Drive-in...

Sometimes we like to go back where fond memories had taken place. For me it was about an hours drive from where I used to live and grew up. The place was still there but the time period was way off which was what I needed to capture again. A restaurant now stood where a drive-in movie used to be. My car stood still in the parking lot and I imagined what year I hoped it to be again. It was a time when a first love was met and shared in the front of a 1963 Chevy convertible. I fell asleep and then awoke to a knock on my driver's side window. A girl on roller skates held a platter of food and drink as she smiled like I was a regular customer. "Did she remember extra ketchup?" The girl sitting next to me said. Maybe she had the same dream as I did as she drove about an hour away from where she used to live. The restaurant was no longer there and a drive-in movie returned to a year of our memories. I made sure there was extra ketchup at our wedding just in case our guests decide to travel away from home....

While You Slept...

You are 500 miles away more or less, but in my dreams you are right next to me. Did you hear the doorbell ring while you slept?

A Toy Soldier...

David was 13 years old and grew up with his mom, a single parent. She told him how his dad was missing in action and presumed dead a year before he was born. Maybe that is why he played with his toy soldiers and made his father part of his life. One Xmas Eve when he was 14 years old he made a special wish to Santa under the tree. Mom tucked him in to bed as both slept soundly that night. The doorbell rang Xmas morning at about 2 am. A former prisoner of war had escaped and made his way back to the state and a home he once lived in. His wife opened the door and they hugged and kissed for what seemed like an eternity. David came out of his room and met dad for the very first time. He held in his hand a toy soldier as dad took it from his son and said "I'm home now." they bonded together as the years that were lost were now captured in a single moment. They all sat around a Xmas tree the following year and exchanged gifts. He hugged his dad when he unwrapped a toy soldier....

3 Feet Above...

I find heaven to be just 3 feet above us and not so far away as we expected it to be. One night as I looked up in a dream, there was my daughter who smiled down upon me and said, "I am ok and happy now," she kissed my cheek just before I woke up. Balloons seemed to be floating in a park I was in which reminded me of how mom and dad used to buy them for me on every one of my birthdays. Nobody saw them except me. They floated just 3 feet above. In my basement apartment I could peek out a window and see the driveway where my car was parked. The engine started by itself and through the driver's side window was the face of my wife who passed away some ten years before. I could hear her voice through the pane of glass saying, "Hi babe I'm home." She kissed my cheek just before I woke up from a window 3 feet above....

A Clear September Morning...

It was A Clear September Morning when the Angels prepared themselves to greet those who were ready. Thick black smoke parted in less than a second to reveal a white loving light where the Angels waited. Passengers from four planes held hands though they were strangers moments before. We all walked together, young and old, to where from whence we came. It was written the night before as his wife had her husband's journal published with this short story included. An Angel smiled at me and pointed to a poem I never thought would be seen. "A Clear September Morning"....

His Name Was Fluffy...

It was Jill's tenth birthday which happened to fall on Xmas Eve. A puppy jumped out of the box that dad had prepared for her ahead of time. He licked her face as she held him in her arms. A connection was instantly established and she gave dad a big hug and kiss for a thank you which was very much appreciated. "This is your new friend and companion, take care of him always," dad said. "I will call him Fluffy," she said to dad. Jill walked him every morning before she went to school and every night. His water and food dish was always full and dad was so proud of how she took care of him. Fluffy slept and curled up with her for many years to come. On her twentieth birthday Fluffy died from natural causes due to old age. She moved out of dad's house and got her own apartment and eventually got married. Sounds of a puppy were heard walking about as she filled a dish of water and food where it used to be. There was a Xmas present in the month of July which didn't make any sense to her why it would be there. A puppy jumped out and licked her face as she held him in her arms. Maybe angels have a way with love and time and seasons to be remembered. The puppy curled up with her in bed and his name was Fluffy. This is a story that follows a dream on loves path....

A Round Trip Ticket...

He stood in the passenger terminal waiting as the passengers left the airplane. His eyes looked at the picture she sent him and then looked at those who entered the lobby. She held a picture of him that he sent and stared at the crowd awaiting their arrival. They spotted each other and for the first time a real kiss was exchanged. He put her suitcase in the trunk of his car as they drove back to his apartment. To talk in person and see each other was a pot of gold at the end of a rainbow. It was during a four day weekend holiday that she stayed with him as they got to know each other. Time flew by so fast as it often does when we are having a good time. He drove her back to the airport as she held her round trip ticket in her hand. Flight 17 is now leaving from New York to Los Angeles, "Have your boarding passes ready for departure," the voice said over the loud speaker. She walked up the ramp to where they board the plane and then turned around to wave goodbye at him. She said to herself, "No, I can't leave him," as she tore up the round trip ticket. He was walking away as she called out his name running down the ramp with her arms extended. They both cried and held each other as tight as one could without ever letting go again. He put her suitcase back in the trunk of his car and drove back to where they finally lived together. A round trip ticket that was torn had a new meaning for those in love. It sent them to a destination not where they were supposed to go, but to a place where they were supposed to return....

On A Labor Day Weekend...

It was Labor Day weekend at a well known resort in Pennsylvania. Somehow there was a mix up in the table arrangements for breakfast that morning and she had nowhere to sit down and eat. My table was empty and I invited her to join me. We introduced ourselves and then ordered from the menu. Funny how we ordered the same thing, something in common this early in the morning was a rare treat. In the early afternoon I sat at a table under an umbrella by the outdoor pool. It was crowded and she had nowhere to sit so I invited her to join me. We both laughed from what happened before and said how strange that this was happening again. The hot sun had us go to the outdoor bar in the pool area as we ordered a drink. Again we ordered the same thing, more in common. She agreed to sit at my table in the dining room for dinner just in case her table was full, which it was. Not to our surprise we ordered the same meal and smiled at each other for more in common. Check out time came at the end of the weekend but we decided to stay another week. We shared a room and found out a lot more about each other. A lot of friends that we met there came back the following year. This time they were guests at our wedding which took place at the outdoor pool. And guess what? She gave birth to a baby boy and girl. Twins on Labor Day weekend. How much more in common can you get? On loves path it happens without us planning. Check out a resort of your own, hopefully in Pennsylvania on a Labor Day weekend....

Pages Of Stories...

The author sold his book to a lady he met at an outdoor pool while both were on vacation. She read a few of his short stories and decided to share it with her 15 year old daughter. Mom never got the book back as the child was deeply moved and read through each story with the intensity that young adults often do. "I want an autograph from this author; can you do that for me mom, please?" "I'll do better than that; you can meet him in person tomorrow by the outdoor pool. I am sure he will be there." He signed the book and she stared at him with a look of something special in her eyes. They got along just fine and met a few times again while staying at the vacation resort that summer. Despite their age differences, they exchanged email addresses and wrote to each other often. The author was totally surprised when one of her mails read, "My English teacher loved the book and now reads one story a day to us kids in class." It was an inspiration from this young teen that had him write a second book. One year later he went back to the same resort as so did the mom and her daughter. "Where Angels Tread," was his second book as mom bought it and immediately passed it on to her daughter. That special look in her eyes returned and he signed the book with a second autograph. He received an email about how her new English teacher loved it and read one story a day to her class. Some years later they met once again without it being planned. She was grown up now and a women of maybe thirty something years old. It was at a book signing event that she stood on line for his third book "On Love's Path." He signed it for her as the two of them walked out of the store holding hands. There was a special look in both of their eyes that somehow was meant to be. Inspiration and love come in many different forms as we grow and understand life. The old and the young meet halfway where autographs and pages of stories connect us....

The Dollhouse...

The babysitter was impressed by the 12 year olds dollhouse. It had three levels with guest rooms, a kitchen, two bathrooms, a living room and kitchen along with 15 dolls that were dressed in their appropriate outfits. She introduced each and every one of them to the babysitter and explained their duties in the house. It was a place of escape in a lonely child's world where the parents weren't home as often as they should be. Emily, the babysitter, played with the little girl and moved the dolls around the house as they all had make- believe conversations with each other. The 25 year old sensed the little girl's loneliness and promised her she would always be her friend. Emily had a favorite doll, the cook and the little girl had her favorite the chauffeur. Mom and dad came home but didn't see the babysitter or their little girl. They called the police as two missing persons were filed in their report. Down the road a bit and maybe in a different town or time a chauffeur opened the back door of his limo. He parked by a shopping mall as he and a cook and Emily along with her new friend stepped out. Neglect and lack of love pay a price for a daughter that was once there. Loneliness and compassion had two people together in a place where they were supposed to be. Emily and the little girl live together along with a cook and a chauffeur in a three level house where those mentioned are now married. The cops examined the dollhouse and found the cook and chauffeur dolls to be missing....

The Fan...

I got a phone call from a distraught dad about his daughter. This is what he said... "My little girl is sick with an incurable disease and asked me to contact you for a football she wants to have signed. She has been a fan of yours for many years and would like to meet you in person. Here is my phone number and address, please call me back. The message on my answering machine touched my heart and I responded immediately with a return call to her dad. The drive was 50 miles away and I arrived at the hospital as her dad met me in the lobby. We got on the elevator and went to the third floor as her room was just two doors down the hall. Her pale face lit up as she spoke with a twinkle in her eye. "Thank you for coming here, my hero; I am your biggest fan." Dad smiled at me for giving her a dozen roses as the room lit up with love and compassion. I signed the football and said to her, "Make me a promise that you will get well again and I'll make sure you have free tickets to every one of our games." She kissed me on the cheek and said, "I'll do my best." It was the following year when we made it to the Super Bowl and at halftime the coach gave his usual speech. She came in with a dozen roses as the locker room suddenly became silent. Dad smiled when he heard us both say, "I love you." He was the best man at our wedding a few months later as at least 24 roses were exchanged. Medicine and doctors and who predict the future failed this time. Something more important was on loves path we never know what is in store for us. Sometimes it's just a fan....

In Between...

It was a simple meeting at an Italian restaurant where I was to meet my bride to be. You might say it was a pre-celebration where both sides of our family would be together and get to know each other. All went well that night in Brooklyn until about 10 pm. Four men entered the restaurant with shotguns and blasted away at a mob boss who was to be eliminated from a local crime family. 5 innocent customers were wounded and 3 were killed that night. My bride to be was one of them. Fast forward to twenty years later as I drove back to the place where it all happened. "Your reservation has been changed to a different night and time," the manager said. "What are you talking about, I just arrived here and made no reservations," I replied. My wife to be and our guests arrived as scheduled on a different date and time. We read the newspapers about a gang shooting the night before and thanked God we weren't there at the time. We got married as planned the next week where time and a second chance had something to do with it. Don't ask me how or why this happened, I just know that it did. You can fast forward and rewind and sometimes capture something in between....

Its Own Destination...

She looked about sixteen or seventeen years old. I would see her getting into and out of cars on my way to work and on my way home. She usually waved at me and I waved back as that was a familiar scene for about a few months. Just two strangers acknowledging each others presence. "How much for your services?" I asked. "It depends on what you want," she replied. "I need two hours of your time and I'll give you five hundred dollars." "You got a deal mister," she said with a smile. We sat in my living room and talked as twenty minutes went by and she asked, "So what you want to do"? "Just talk to you and listen," I replied. "It's your money mister, go ahead and speak what's on your mind." After the two hours she seemed to feel better, spilling her life's miseries and downfalls. "You know mister, I never had a friend or a father that cared about me the way you do." "Feel free to visit me anytime," I replied. Her trips in and out of cars with strangers became less frequent as a lot of her time was spent with me. It was out of love a few months later that it happened for us and not for money. She was absolutely beautiful in a white wedding gown that replaced worn jeans and a torn tee shirt. It's only my car that she gets in and out of now, for loves path has a way of finding its own destination....

It Was A Place...

It was a place where lonely people went for a last chance or maybe a last call. To meet that special someone or just kill time before the next day was to begin again. Up we go again a flight of stairs and knock on a door which is called "After Hours." I found an empty stool at the bar and ordered a drink which was just out of habit. The painted black windows blocked out the morning sun as it still felt like night time. My lighter dropped to the floor before I could light my cigarette but a match from the person next to me lit it up. We said hello to each other and talked about how to solve the world's problems. I took a few quarters off the counter from my change and walked over to the jukebox in the back left corner of the room. She followed me there and our fingers pressed the same button of our favorite old slow song. I remember waking up next to her at a place that must have been where she lived. A fading memory of a slow dance and promises of us always being together had surfaced to my now sober mind. About two years later our guests arrived at a beautiful wedding ceremony. The bartender was there and a few regulars from that old place we used to hang out at. It was just before noon when we walked up a flight of stairs as the photographer snapped our pictures. An old jukebox sat in the back left corner of the room. She followed behind me and then placed her finger over mine as we pressed our favorite old slow song. On love's path we see through blackened out windows and a staircase of dreams that sometimes comes true....

Michelle...

She browsed the fiction section in her local library and picked out two books by the same author. It wasn't just the titles that caught her eye, but his description on the back cover that interested her most, along with his photo. In the course of six months she read both books at least three times. There were stories that touched her very deeply and she looked up his name on the computer to find his address. All she wanted was for him to sign both books which she later bought at a book store in her neighborhood. Michelle rang his doorbell and introduced herself as a big fan who just wanted his autograph. "Incredible Short Stories" was signed and the second book "Where Angels Tread" was signed also. They talked of private and personal things in their lives over a dinner he made for her. The writer and the reader started dating shortly after. There was love and passion between the two and an understanding of matters of the heart. It was about one year later when he surprised Michelle with his third book. "Turn to the last page my darling," he said. It read as follows..."and so two who have never met before inspired each other in a way that rarely happens in real life." After reading that she kissed him goodnight and went to sleep. In the morning she closed the book that lay beside her and then turned it over to the cover which showed the title "Michelle". It made the best seller list as they both autographed a marriage license a week later. Sometimes a library and a fan and a writer have something in common. Lessons to be learned in our daily lives....

In Between The Lines...

It was recommended by a friend who read his first book by a chance stop at the local book store. The subject was fiction, but for many it was as real as it gets when the readers related the short stories to their own lives. His second book had the same effect though with a different title, it expressed emotions and desires that we all can relate to. In between the lines was something more than just words printed on each page of his book. It made those readers think and wonder and hope of things that could have or possibly would happen. A smiling picture of the author on the back of both books along with a description of its contents made each sale final. The age group ranged from 15 to 65 and older as each reader could relate to its contents. His third book was dedicated to all of the readers and fans who he had loved from the beginning. There were many book signings and events that took place over the years as it all started by a friend who recommended it. A stranger stared at him while at the local supermarket in between the lines. She was his first fan many years ago and approached him outside the store. "I carried your books everywhere I went hoping to get an autograph and run into you in person," she said. He smiled again just like the photo on the back of each book and signed his name inside the front cover of all three of his books. Somewhere in between the lines there was something read and something written just for her. It was called "The Parking Lot, Where We Met." So a fictional story from his third book came true. We find love when not looking for it and sometimes it happens in between the lines....

May Old Acquaintances...

I walked through the tunnel and wondered where I was and how I got there. Mom and dad said hello and I kept walking towards the light. Old friends and pets smiled at me as if it was yesterday. There was a warm loving feeling with no fear whatsoever as I continued towards the light. I had to sign in at the end of the tunnel and then was instructed to attend an orientation class. The teacher explained how we all died and left the earth plane and what we have to do over here on the other side. There were museums and libraries and other things that we once knew still existed. I met for the second time my first love and many people who had passed on that shared their same experiences. Old acquaintances never forgotten. There were portals where we could go back to earth and visit our favorite places that we left behind. Each of us had a job to perform as we did on earth and so our choosing would determine our heavenly salary. I chose to write as I did before. Not much money there but the reward of knowing that others were touched was enough for me. An angel came to me and said "because of your heart and love for others you have a choice to stay here or return to the earth plane." I looked behind me and said a temporary goodbye to old acquaintances that I would be seeing again. A nurse pounded on my chest as my heart beat once again. "Welcome back," she said as my first girlfriend wore a uniform that she once wore on the earth plane. We held hands while in orientation knowing that we would never be separated. May old acquaintances....

On My Lap...

My voice was her voice as she sat on my lap when I made the crowd laugh. Betty was my little figure of a doll that sat there and responded as we exchanged jokes and argued back and forth. My profession was a ventriloquist and she was no dummy for sure. Sometimes I thought she had a mind of her own when she would talk to me while I was asleep. One last performance before I retired was in a sold out house at Madison Square Garden. The crowd stood on its feet as they laughed and cheered my last farewell. She sat in the attic of my home in a box with things stored away from previous years. The ad in the paper was answered for the sale of my house as she entered the front door. Familiar blue eyes with blonde hair spoke to me and said, "Remember me?" My name is Betty. We argued as usual and exchanged jokes but this time it was not in front of an audience. My dummy was no longer in a box stored in the attic, but right there in front of me. Betty got a ring that night which stated that we were engaged to be married. Who knew that wood and flesh and blood would be the same? Sometimes love is not just between us regular people, but for those who need it the most. The wedding went as planned and the priest blessed our marriage even though it happened while she sat on my lap....

It Was A Chance...

It was a chance he took when his car drove over a hundred miles for a surprise visit. One hand rang the bell and the other held a dozen roses. "Sorry sir, but she moved out of here about a month ago," he said. The flowers wilted in the back seat on his way home. It was a chance she took when her car drove over a hundred miles for a surprise visit. One hand rang the bell and the other held a dozen roses. "Sorry miss, but he moved out of here about a month ago," she said. The flowers wilted in the back seat on her way home. In between about 50 miles they lived together in a town where people eventually get to know each other. They met in a flower shop for the first time and finally said hello in person. Each bought a single red rose and handed it to one another as they kissed as it was meant to be. She moved in with him and the distance of love was now only a pillow away. The following Xmas Eve she opened a little black box and put the engagement ring on her finger. We travel some miles to be disappointed and then meet half way unexpectedly. For those who wish to meet, let me suggest a dozen roses and a single one where we meet halfway. It was a chance....

A Table For Two...

I made reservations for a table for two but she never showed up. And so it became just me and dinner for one. The waitress smiled on a weekly basis and sat me down in the usual spot until she was off duty and joined me for a drink. She became a customer as she quit the job and made future reservations for us. It turned out she left living with her parents and moved in with me in a basement apartment not to far away from the diner she used to work at. By a stroke of luck she won a lottery of 500,000 dollars and we bought a home just five miles out of town. One Saturday night we sat at a table for two where she used to work and I used to cry. A ring made it official and the following year we got married. Some twenty years later our daughter served tables at a diner my wife used to work at. Someone never showed up as he sat alone until she sat down with him while she was off duty. She quit the job and made future reservations for the both of them our daughter moved out and lived with him in a basement apartment not too far away. A ring fit and the wife and I attended their wedding. We smiled at our own experiences and how our daughter went through the same way. Life has a way where we enter and leave diners where reservations end up at a table for two....

The Campfire...

The hotel was closed during November and December as I went back there to visit. No need to check-in; just visit a place I had been to before as a kid some forty years ago. Why I came back was to capture a moment in time that never left my memory. It was clear as if it was yesterday when I sat at a campfire and listened to ghost stories from the camp counselor as we all held hands in a circle of fear. She put her arms around my neck and the comfort was for both of us. We kissed before it was time to go back to our rooms as the curfew was over for us ten to thirteen year olds. I lit some old wood and placed it in the middle of the stones and wished I was back there again. You might say it was a first love or crush, or whatever. Someone else had the same idea as she visited a hotel she once stayed at some forty years ago. Behind me I could hear footsteps and turned around to see a familiar face. She smiled and sat next to me as we held hands once again. We kissed as adults this time and there was no curfew here we had to obey. The hotel opened that following summer and we checked in together. About 250 guests arrived at an outdoor wedding where my childhood sweetheart and I got married. A lot of the guests there sat around the campfire and held hands. Some even hugged and kissed. In the future quite a few kids went back during November and December to visit a childhood memory. Needless to say it all started around the campfire....

Can You Hear The Bell Ring...

I could hear the bell ring down the street from inside my house. The white truck stopped in the middle of the block at three o'clock in the afternoon every day during the week. It was during June, July, and August that the Good Humor man would make his daily rounds. Mom gave me a dollar bill and reminded me to bring back the change. It was either a vanilla pop or a twin fudge icicle as the Good Humor man would reach into the door and pull it out. My neighbor Jenny would often be behind me on line and sometimes she was short of change to pay for herself. Mom laughed as there was no change to give her as she said, "I guess you treated Jenny again." These were fond memories of maybe forty years ago which always stuck in my mind. It was June that I decided to go back to a block I used to live on as a kid. I sat in my car and waited for three o'clock that afternoon. No white truck showed up but I got out my car anyway with a craving for what I once had. A lady stood behind me waiting for the same thing. I took out a dollar bill as Jenny and I remembered something we both came looking for. It was on that same block that our daughter and son heard a bell ring at about three o'clock in the afternoon. We look backward and then find something to look forward to again. Case in point, two kids now adults with a dream shared then and now....

Sometimes When We Write...

A pen scribbles a love note and is placed on a school desk in front of him. She sits down and reads it as the boy behind her watches intently. The ten year old girl turns around and smiles at the boy behind her. A kiss is exchanged before the bell rings to let them out of school. Some ten years later he recognizes that same little girl in the lunch room where they eventually wound up together at the same place of work. He scribbled a note and left it on the table in front of him where she sat. "You may not remember me but it was ten years ago that you read my first note in the school we used to go to. I'll never forget when you turned around and smiled. I'll never forget that first kiss." She sat back down and read the note as he watched intensely. She called my name and remembered me as her next smile was more beautiful than the first. A second kiss was more passionate and we talked for a long time. Eventually we moved out of our parents homes and decided to share an apartment together. I wrote her a note at the kitchen table while she was in the bathroom. She came back and sat down and read what I left her. She faced me this time with no need to turn around and replied "yes, I will marry you." We both sat and scribbled out invitations to our wedding for the following summer. On loves path it may take a day or a month or some years. It doesn't really matter as long as the results are the same. Sometimes when we write....

Another Pillow...

I hear a favorite old song and slow dance with you. One match lights two candles at dinner time no matter where we sit. Our glasses click in a toast with no occasion necessary except for just being with you. My pillow is empty without you, but my dreams have you there. The answering machine left a message but I was never home. Can we get together this time? Hold one match and save our glasses. Put another pillow beside you....

A Deck Of 52...

A cruise to the Bahamas Islands for 7 days and 7 nights had Michael smile as he boarded the huge luxury ship. The cabin was comfortable and convenient, one flight below the top deck and one flight above the bar and restaurant and dance floor. The morning sun gave way to an early afternoon trip to the lounges on the upper deck where he sat by the pool. Just for the fun of it and out of curiosity he counted the people there. It was a deck of 52. Michael pulled some cards and started to play solitaire. "Know any other card games we could play together?" The stranger asked. He told her of a few and they agreed on a game of 500 rummy. They went swimming afterwards and talked in the pool as they got to know each other. Carol had a room next to his on the lower deck, coincidence or fate may be decided by the readers of this story. That night was a date to meet for dinner, drinks, and dancing. It was time spent together for the entire 7 days and 7 nights that two people had the best times of their lives. They spent nights in each others cabins and made love while others just slept. Next year they boarded the same cruise with a perfect timing of a seven day honeymoon. Nobody thought about it at the time except for me, the writer of this love story. The guests at this wedding consisted of a deck of 52....

To Treat Others...

Her name cannot be pronounced because she is an angel. Born of God and only known to those in heaven. She requested to be in human form and live as a human on earth to learn more and feel what they feel. God touched her wings and they became arms as He said "go now and live on earth." She was 25 years old and her name was Sharon. Walking the streets as a prostitute she had no memory of once being an angel and so her life on earth began experiencing what down and out was about. Robert talked to her and offered 100 dollars for her company over a weekend at his basement apartment. She accepted. They spoke all night with no sex involved and she wondered why this man was so interested in her. "Move in with me please," he said after a few months seeing each other. There was something special about him that showed a genuine caring for another human being and Sharon accepted his proposal. There were no more other men for money and sex as Robert took care of her emotionally, physically, and spiritually. He asked her to be his bride and a wedding took place one year later. In a dream God appeared to her and asked "so what did you find out about this human experience?" She told Him that despite all the evil in the world, there was one who had a heart of an angel. God smiled down upon the both of them and said in her dream, "What do you wish to do now?" I want to return to heaven as the angel I used to be, but can he come with me?" God replaced his arms with wings as so deserved. Both Sharon and Robert stood before Him back in heaven. "The both of you have learned valuable lessons and shall earn new names as you and he will spread your new wings and fly once again together." In between two worlds we travel and learn what we have to. The outcome is how we decide to treat others....

Odette...

The nineteen year old maid took care of a huge house that was owned by a rich plantation owner. It took place during the late 1800's in the south where slavery and prejudice were common for the times. Odette was her name and she was accused by rumors that she slept with the white man who owned the plantation where she worked. The thirty five year old Michael was also a lawyer and proceeded to defend his maid in court. She was found not guilty but the town residents wanted their own form of justice, an old fashioned hanging. While her master was away an angry mob stormed the house and dragged Odette to the nearest tree. They put a rope around her neck as her master came home and approached the mob. "Would you kill also the unborn baby that lies within her belly?" He shouted. "There is an innocent life here involved that should not be denied its place in this world." The anger and prejudice left the faces of those who hated as they thought about their own young children. Odette was let down and the knot became untied from around her neck. Michael held up a ring in front of the now docile crowd and said "This is what I plan to do, marry her as not to make this whole affair something hidden and disgusting." He put it on her finger and she smiled with a yes for her reply. A small town where prejudice and hate once resided now became one of tolerance and compassion. A lesson to be learned from the past which hopefully continues into the present and future. My name is Michael now living in the year of 2,009. I hired a maid in my small two bedroom apartment. She introduced herself as Odette....

Out Of The Woods...

The forest was quiet and peaceful, lush green trees with sunlight peaking through the leaves. Winding paths and hills to climb took most of the day as I settled down to rest for awhile. My sleeping bag was now ready as sunset dimmed the woods around me. The second day had me lost as my mistake was just relying on memory of which way to get back to the place I started from. A deer caught my attention and walked off a ways until she turned around again to see if I would follow her. Through the winding paths and hills to descend, I followed her to a road where I first started my journey. How did this animal lead me to safety and out of the woods once again? A lady stood beside her car parked just inside the road that led to the forest. "Need a ride?" the stranger said. "Yes, thank you so much. I live just about an hour away." She drove me home and I invited her in to thank her for saving my life. She seemed a little lost herself and told me about where she used to live. It rained that night and she left in the morning as we both agreed to see each other again. Her footprints were clear until they reached the edge of a forest about an hour away. They became that of a deer which was not for me to see. As promised we did get back together again and eventually became lovers and friends. She accepted my proposal of marriage and we often take hikes in the woods together. Maybe in nature both have been lost and found. In what form or shape doesn't really matter you see. On loves path we all eventually come out of the woods....

A Calendar Of Choice...

It was attached to his fridge by a magnet that displayed all of the months and days of the year. Nothing was circled or checked off to remind him of things to do or places to visit. He did however take a pen and scratch in a minus sign on all of the holidays that he spent alone. Not too far away from him she puts check marks on events and things to do on a calendar attached to her fridge by a magnet. The holidays were filled and booked up as she smiled. On Xmas Eve they ran into each other at the local liquor store to buy what they needed, both for different reasons. For her to celebrate, for him to drown the sorrows of loneliness. "Hello," she said with a smile as they checked out together on the short line. "Can I walk with you for a while until you get home?" he asked. They talked for about five blocks before she had to go her way and he his way. She felt his being alone and turned around when he walked away. "Hey, wait a minute, you can come to our Xmas party if you feel like it," she said. He shook his head yes with a tear running down his cheek that she wiped away with a kiss. They held hands when they walked into her parent's house and she introduced her new found friend. Mom and dad liked the young man and so he felt comfortable and wanted. New Years Eve had them clicking glasses and wishing each other a Happy New Year. Those who have plans and those who do not finally met where loneliness and happiness met halfway in between. A few months later they shared the same apartment as a magnet held a calendar on their fridge. He took a pen for the first time and circled a date for when they were to be married. It was a calendar of choice....

The Edge Of Daylight...

The edge of daylight peeked through her bedroom window at sunrise one Saturday morning. Caroline rubbed her eyes and slowly made her way into the kitchen to fix some coffee. She kissed the portrait photo that sat on the table that reminded her of a husband missing in action some ten years before. Anthony awoke from a coma in a hospital a few miles away and wondered how he got there in the first place. His last memory was in a thick forest with a loud gunshot just as the sun came up. That was ten years ago. The doctor handed him a photo, the only possession found on him at the edge of daylight in front of the emergency room. He knew the name of Caroline but wasn't sure how they knew each other. After rehabilitation he left the hospital and called for a taxi. His unconscious mind told the driver where to go as he had no idea why. It was a Saturday morning as the edge of daylight peeked through the front windshield of the taxi cab. Anthony held an old photo in his hand and knocked on the door. She rubbed the sleep from her eyes and went past the kitchen to open the front door. "Caroline?" he asked. She cried and shouted "my Anthony, where have you been?" It all came back to him in flooding memories of what once was. It was Sunday morning where they made love the night before as they did so many times, so many years ago. We forget and remember with love and hope in our hearts. Case in point of Caroline and Anthony, who recaptured the edge of daylight....

The Planetarium...

It was a school trip on a Saturday afternoon to the planetarium. We eighth graders sat in our seats in random order around the circular rotunda. The lights went out as a display lit the dome above our heads. Shooting stars and falling comets started the show as a voice from a speaker narrated what was about to happen. It was the best 45 minutes I had ever spent in my young life as two minutes before it ended a classmate and I were holding hands. This was a memory from 1956 that always stayed with me. Twenty years later the planetarium was still there and it was on a Saturday that the urge to go back there hit me. I sat in a random seat and waited for a familiar voice to come over the speakers. About two minutes before the show was over, I felt a hand hold mine. She was an eighth grader who remembered the last two minutes and wondered some twenty years later who it was, just like I did. We kissed for the first time and knew who each other was from a childhood memory that had us get together again. On a Saturday night while we vacationed in the mountains together, we lay down on the grass and stared up at the stars. A voice narrated the events to come as he said "do you take this man for your husband?" she said "yes." Do you take this woman for your wife?" he said "yes." In life we find a place to go back to. Sometimes it may be indoors or outdoors. In the case of two dreamers from eighth grade, it was the planetarium....

A Tissue And A Song...

We sat in the movie theater during a love story as a song played which touched us both. My girlfriend opened her pocketbook and took out a few tissues which she shared with me. The ending was sad but nonetheless it was a fantastic movie. High school sweethearts often part ways never to be seen again, but in this story we met again. Fast forward to fifteen years later in a local club where by chance or fate we met again. About ten minutes before closing I went to the jukebox and noticed a song from a movie soundtrack a long time ago. It was "The Rose" It had me think of a girl I used to love back then and I put a quarter in and pressed the button. "Remember me?" She asked as the song played once again. We made the most out of those last ten minutes and slow danced as if there was nobody else in the room. She opened her pocketbook and shared some tissues which were needed once again. Some say love, it is a river, that drowns the tender reed. I say love it is a razor that leaves your soul to bleed. Some say love, it is a hunger, an endless aching need. I say love, it is a flower, and you it's only seed. Both our parents were happy to see us get together again after all these years and paid for a beautiful wedding that took place a year later. The live band played a song from a movie and a jukebox where we met for the second time. We danced and kissed on the floor when her mom brought my wife's pocketbook to her and took some tissues. We both cried again along with most of the guests which happens at a lot of weddings. For those who believe, let me submit a tissue and a song....

Cabin Number Five...

The lake was quiet and I paddled under a full moon with the sound of crickets lulling me to sleep. It was in the middle of a small resort where my week's vacation started and ended abruptly. About fifty feet from shore I fell asleep and leaned over a bit too much, my body went overboard and hit the water. It woke me up but water filled my lungs before I could reach the surface. My next memory was being put on a stretcher and placed in an ambulance and driven to a hospital. A visitor came into my room when I recovered and told me how she saved my life. She was a guest in cabin number five. Her eyes were like that of an angel with a voice that sounded like it came from heaven. "What can I do to repay you for saving my life?" I asked. "Take me on a ride in a canoe on a lake with a full moon above and crickets singing," she replied. We did that the following summer and fell in love maybe for the second time. She said yes to my proposal of marriage as my angel and I planned out a honeymoon trip on a cruise to the Bahamas the following summer. I look back now some twenty years later and wonder if this all was a coincidence or a sign of something very special. In my mind and heart it was something very special. On the middle deck of the ship, the captain led us to our room. It was cabin number five....

Balloons And Birthday Candles...

Balloons and birthday candles made my day very special at my parent's house this particular Saturday night. I had just turned ten years old as friends from the block we lived on sat around the kitchen table and celebrated it with me. Mom and dad answered a knock on the door where two parents stood there with their nine year old daughter. "We heard that your son was having a party and even though our daughter wasn't invited, we would appreciate it if you let her join in." "Certainly," mom and dad said. "Please come in." She was a girl I had a secret crush on from school and was really excited to see her at my party. Susan told me that her birthday was on the same day as mine, but she wanted to be here with me. My heart jumped to my throat as I thought to myself the girl of my dreams actually wanted to be with me. She was the last guest to leave my party but not without a special goodbye. It was a kiss that stayed in my memory for the next fifteen years. We attended the same high school but didn't know it and never ran into each other. At the prom graduation dance our eyes met and recognized each other from so many years ago. We had the last slow dance together and another kiss which was much more serious this time around. I knocked on her door and said "Happy birthday sweetheart." Our wedding ceremony had two things which brought us together in the first place. The date was on the same day we were born as balloons and birthday candles made it a special occasion....

A Small Midwestern State...

There was a small Midwestern state I grew up in for the first twenty one years of my life. A small town of maybe three hundred people if I remember correctly. The plane touched down at the small airport just about twenty miles from where I used to live. My thoughts were of a church where I used to be a choir boy that brought back so many fond memories. These fifty year old legs walked through now what was a ghost town. Just down the road was the chapel faded in red paint with broken windows and a few chipped concrete steps leading to the front door. It creaked open and the rows of seats still stood there with some dust and cobwebs. On both sides of the pulpit my eyes became teary when from my memory I could see the boys and girls choir singing their praises. We looked at each other when we were 18 and 17 back then with loving eyes, but never got together. A plane landed and she walked into a ghost town and proceeded up a few chipped concrete steps leading to the front door. Her forty nine year old legs walked past the benches down the center aisle as she looked to left and then to right. The sun shone through some faded stained glass broken windows as a figure on a cross smiled down upon us. We sang once again and stared at each other with loving eyes. This time we never touch with each other and as a matter of fact, got married in that same church some three years later. Time and distance traveled on loves path in a small Midwestern state where we now live together....

The Edge Of The Platform...

Mandy stepped to the edge of the platform and looked to the right through a tunnel for the next train. She wasn't waiting to travel like most of us, but decided to end her life by jumping onto the tracks. The 40 year old depressed lady got her wish when she saw the train's headlights about 500 feet away. Mandy jumped and curled up on the tracks below waiting for her death wish. I was standing next to her and without thinking jumped down and tried to pick up the unconscious body as the sound of a loud blasting horn came out of the tunnel. Sparks flew on the tracks as the brakes were applied when I picked her up and rested her on the platform above me. Another onlooker grabbed my hand and pulled me up as the train came to a screeching hall about 20 feet from where we both would have been crushed to death. Mandy awoke in the same hospital as me and during our recovery we got to talk for the first time. "Why am I here and why did you save me?" She asked. "Because I didn't want you to miss your next stop," I replied. She laughed out loud and said "you know, maybe you had a good idea." It turned out that we had a lot in common and dated for the next two years. We live together now but don't take the train to work anymore. Sometimes we meet a stranger under life threatening circumstances and both survive for reasons unknown to us at the present time. It wasn't their time to go, but to stay. This is a story about my mom and dad which I am proud to write about. You see, I am here at the edge of the platform....

Garage Sale...

I went to a garage sale down the block and saw just what I needed. It was a 20 foot long garden hose which my house never came with. The young lady sold it to me and I attached it to the appropriate outlet in my back yard. Some months later I needed some cash and set up a garage sale of my own. She smiled at me and said "well, it looks like now I am going to buy from you." We both laughed. She was interested in some planters and soil included along with flower pots for her back yard. She paid me and went back to her outdoor garden. The following summer weekend I went to water my usual planters and then laughed to myself as they were no longer there. My neighbor lady looked at her planters with soil included and then laughed when she realized I had her garden hose. We visited each other often as we joked about our dilemma and decided to move in together. The house we bought came with a garden hose and planters with soil included in our new back yard. Maybe neighbors with something to sell and buy have more in common than what they think. A small walk just down the street had those two get together on loves path. In this story, it was just a garage sale....

Blue Star Sapphire...

In the middle of my gold high school ring was a blue star sapphire. Inside was inscribed "love me always." This was a surprise gift for a high school sweetheart after our graduation in the summer of 1965. I put it on her finger while we sat on a blanket beneath a boardwalk at a beach we often went to. For us it was a symbol just like an engagement ring for a couple to be married. Maybe it was a little loose on her finger or maybe the waves of the ocean had it separated from her. We didn't notice that it was missing until the next morning. She cried over the phone as my love told me it was lost. Such was the memory of twenty years ago which haunted me in dreams and waking hours. The beach was only about an hour away from where I now lived and my heart told me to drive there once again. Under the same boardwalk I sat with the original blanket I saved for reasons of my own. Just about five feet in front of me a wave rested at my toes with the full moon shining on a blue star sapphire. The year was the same as also an inscription "love me always". She drove to a beach about an hour away from where she now lived. "Do I know you sir? Your blanket looks so familiar to me," she said. I looked her in the eyes and said, "It's been a long time but yes, you do know me for sure." I placed the ring on her finger once again as she smiled and cried when we kissed and made love for the second time. I'm not sure what year it was when this happened but it doesn't really matter. Maybe an inscription of "love me always" had something to do with it. The wedding hall had a strange name to it but was very appropriate at the time. "Blue Star Sapphire"....

20 Miles To Las Vegas...

The needle swung to the left and read that the gas tank was empty. My luck wasn't any better when smoke rose from under the hood as the engine overheated. Next to me was my destination, a sign that read "Las Vegas 20 miles ahead." There was nothing but desert on the right and left of the highway so I opened the trunk and took out the one suitcase I had. My right hand held it and my left hand had a thumb up for maybe a ride that would save a 20 mile walk. The sound of a horn was a beautiful wake up call after 5 miles of walking in the desert heat. She just picked up my suitcase and put it in the back seat of her car and said "need a ride to Las Vegas?" A big hug to her was a response that she took as yes. It was strange that we had a reservation at the same hotel at the same time, but I was thankful for that and so was she after we checked in together. Originally our vacation was planned to be alone, but the company we shared together made the two weeks that much more pleasant. There was a promise that we would get together again sometime in the future as we kissed each other goodbye. Five years later the needle swung to the left and read that the gas tank was empty. Her luck wasn't any better when smoke rose from under the hood as the engine overheated. I saw her carry a suitcase in her right hand as her left had a thumb up. She hugged me with a welcome smile and I drove her about 20 miles to Las Vegas. The road that we traveled before somehow met again and that was all we needed you see. This time our vacation wasn't to be alone, but together not only for the second time, but for the rest of our lives....

Waiting On Line...

While waiting on line at the post office, the lady in front of me fumbled through her purse looking for her wallet. She cursed out loud for leaving it at home with no money to pay for the package she wanted to be delivered. After waiting there for about 30 minutes, I felt she shouldn't be turned away, so I offered to pay for her. A few days later at a local nightclub I saw her standing on line waiting to get into the ladies room. I snuck her into the men's room as it was empty and stood outside waiting for her to finish. We finally said hello and introduced ourselves as we walked back upstairs and shared a few drinks together. One Saturday the next month I felt a tap on my shoulder while waiting on line to get into a movie theater. Sitting alone which was originally our plan had become watching the movie together. We talked about these strange unexpected meetings and how it may be significant for the future. In the coming weeks and months we never stood behind or in front of each other. We always stood side by side. The guests dropped their envelopes on a table in front of us with checks and money as they were waiting on line. Spoons and forks clicked the champagne glasses, a tradition for the bride and groom to give each other a kiss....

Two Halves Make A Whole...

The boredom and routine from day to day was too much to bear for her. The same was with him and they both agreed that she would move to the state where he lived. It was a chance to take as each accepted something more than the way things were going at the time. Now in their 50's it was either do or die so to speak. She rented a room according to the budget and it was a perfect ten minutes away from where he lived. They got together for the first time as words were now finally said in person as opposed to the letters typed in on a computer some hundreds of miles away. A real hug and kiss were exchanged and then the two of them shared each others dreams and desires. You might say "two halves make a whole." Eventually she saved up and got her own apartment, this time about five minutes away from where he lived. The distance grew closer not only in miles, but in matters of the heart. She took to his house a box of pizza that was half finished and thought he would like the rest of it. In a strange coincidence he saved his box of half a pie for her also that evening. You might say "two halves make a whole." An engagement ring was placed on her finger and she said, "Yes, I will marry you." The bride cut the wedding cake as they shared and fed each other from that moment on. "Two halves make a whole"....

A Tear For Humanity...

It wasn't a bum that I talked to who slept on a park bench, but another human being who just was homeless. His story was a sad one of how his divorced wife took his home, his children, and eventually his job. We sat on his bench and shared some breakfast and hot coffee that winter in the weeks that followed. Eventually he cleaned up his act and began working for me in a decent paying job that I had found for him. You might say it was a tear for humanity. A prostitute approached my car at a red light as they often do in the neighborhood I drive through on the way home from work. It was a Friday evening and I told her to get in. Five hundred dollars was my offer for a weekend together at my home and she agreed. After the first night she asked "No sex? You just want to talk?" I nodded yes and she said "It's your money mister." She opened up her life story about an abusive father who she grew up with and a drug addicted mother. The black eye and bruises eventually healed along with her thoughts of the lifestyle she was living in. We lived together in my home and she became a respected person who was finally treated the way she should be. She no longer wears hot pink shorts and high heels, but a business suit in a now well known advertising agency. You might say it was a tear for humanity. I sponsored a child from a third world country and exchanged photos and letters for the next two years. Her progress was amazing as she got educated along with proper medical treatment that she needed. Arrangements were made for her to move to the United States and I adopted her at the age of twelve. My life was soon to be over at 72 from heart failure. An angel took me home and reviewed my life and said to me "On loves path you have traveled and made a difference in others. There are a few people here who would like to say hello to you again." A once homeless man sat with me as he treated me to breakfast and coffee. A former prostitute in a business suit had me stay at her place for a few months as we talked of old times together. My daughter put her arms around my neck and said "Welcome home daddy." His wings spread wide as the Angel submitted a tear for humanity....

The Gardener...

Emily got her divorce and he moved out. She was now sole proprietor of the house. There were no children involved from their two year marriage and no more help was there to tend to the lush garden surrounding her property. She needed to hire a gardener on weekends to do what her husband used to take care of. A reference check with recommendations was performed as the interview proceeded with positive results. He was hired for Saturdays from nine am to eleven am and on Sundays from two pm till four pm. The garden bloomed with spring and summer flowers the way it used to be before her divorce. Sometimes he would drive her to places she needed to go to on those weekends as she had no car of her own. It was just a favor he did for Emily without extra pay. He showed up one Monday morning as she was leaving for work and said "I know it is not my time to be here but," his words stopped there as he held his shy head down and just extended his hand out to her. A rose picked from her garden was clutched in his hand. Emily was surprised but touched at the same time as she held it up to her nose and sniffed its fragrance. "Even my ex-husband never gave me a flower, let alone a rose," she said. She placed it in a vase that was empty on her nightstand in the bedroom for too many years that were forgotten. Michael did the arrangements in an outdoor garden the following summer. It was there at a wedding ceremony where he handed her a hand picked rose just before the priest blessed their marriage. We travel on loves path sometimes for a second time. Emily looked out her window on many weekends to come to see the gardener....

He Was The First Born...

He was the first born with no brothers or sisters. Growing up was sort of lonely except for the usual outside friends that try to fill the void of an empty home where mom and dad were not home more often than they were. She sat in front of him in classes from grade school to high school until he finally spoke to her with a single red rose and a tear in his eye. There was much in common as she was an only child also and they talked like a brother and a sister that was missing in their younger years. This was a friendship that lasted through the college years until he handed her a rose with a new intention this time. A kiss before on the cheek was now on the lips. Growing up was no longer lonely now as outside friends suddenly became someone on the inside. He met her at work on a coffee break and handed her a single red rose with a special card attached. "I love you, will you marry me?" She screamed, "Yes, I will my darling." There was a round of applause from workers who were in distance of listening to them. I stood in the room and held her hand as the doctors told her to push. He was the first born....

To Come Home To...

And so there is a memory of something from childhood that stays with us. For me it was sitting around a campfire holding hands with other kids while the counselor told ghost stories. My watch read seven pm that evening of July seventh in the year of 1961. It was two scared twelve olds who held hands and kissed each other for the first time. That was the first time I met Rebecca and I wondered about her ever since. In 1981 I traveled back there during the off season to recapture that treasured memory. Some old stones surrounded what used to be a place we sat before. I gathered some twigs and lit a fire during that cold November evening. Rebecca reflected upon a memory from childhood when she was twelve years old. It was of holding hands and a first kiss that had her wonder about me ever since. It was during the off season about the same time and year that I thought about her also. "Michael?" she asked from a few feet behind me. We held hands and kissed for the second time where dreams and memories connect once again for real. The following summer there was an outdoor wedding at a camp site where stones still sit around a camp fire for those who wish to come back to....

Teddy And Blanket...

There was a brown teddy bear and a yellow blanket that my son could not sleep without. One little hand held teddy next to him and the other clutched his blanket as I kissed him goodnight. In later years we played with his toy cars and soldiers and then we threw the football and baseball back and forth followed by a "goodnight son, I love you." Teenage years soon came and new friends had him sort of forget that dad was still here. Teddy and blanket were saved in a curio cabinet in the living room as a live reminder that photos somehow lose. A drunk driver killed my son just after high school graduation and I wondered how and why. We are supposed to pass on before our children, not them before us. A heart attack had me wake in a hospital bed maybe a week or two later. A young man in a graduation suit entered my room while I slept and told me how much he missed me and that he loved me and never forgot about the times growing up with his dad. One of my hands held teddy next to me as the other clutched a yellow blanket. We threw the football and baseball around once again in a special place where heaven has us once again together. The curio cabinet in the living room had all the items in place except for teddy and blanket....

Fifth On Line...

Down the flight of steps he walked slowly to reach the restrooms one level below the bar. The young man did his thing with a sigh of relief and went back out into the small hallway. Five young ladies stood there on a line waiting to get into where they had to go. The men's room was empty at the time and he spoke to the fifth girl just in front of him. "Excuse me miss, you can go in here and I'll stand watch outside until you are finished." She kissed him on the cheek as a thank you and did her thing with a sigh of relief. He waited in the small hallway until she returned and then introduced himself. The young lady was glad that he was still there and she also spoke her name which now made the introduction official. Four feet walked back up the stairs while holding hands to the main bar area. It was just a kind gesture on his part back in 1978 which stood in his mind some ten years later. He often thought about her and wondered if they would ever meet again. Maybe she thought the same thing. A different crowd attended in 1988 but there still remained a staircase to a lower level where the bathrooms still remained. She did her business and returned out back to the small hallway. Her head turned around to see an older young man standing fifth in line waiting to get into the men's room. "Excuse me sir, you can go in here and I'll stand watch outside until you are finished." He kissed her on the cheek as a thank you and did his thing with a sigh of relief. "Have we met before?" they both said at the same time. Their names were very familiar as a sudden memory and longing had them hold hands once again as they walked back up the stairs to the main bar area. Both stood before the reception area of a hall that was to be rented for a wedding. They were the fifth on line....

An Aisle Remembered...

It was unusually quiet for a Saturday afternoon at the local supermarket. Neither one of them paid attention as they pushed their carts down the same aisles while heading towards each other. A head on crash had their shopping minds jolted back to reality. They looked at each other, laughed out loud as there was no other traffic in their aisle. Each continued on and eventually met on the same line at the checkout counter. She stood in front of him and fumbled through her wallet for a credit card that was left at home. "After all that aisle walking, it would be a shame to leave here without your stuff," he said. The kind thoughtful gentleman handed the cashier his credit card and said "it's on me." She was shocked and surprised how a total stranger would bail her out of such an embarrassing situation. "I will pay you back if you follow me home, I have the cash back there," she said with a thankful smile. He entered her home and she asked him to wait there in the kitchen while she got the money. 20, 40, 60, 80, 100, 120 was handed to him in twenty dollar bills. "A deed done without repayment is a reward unto itself," he said. "Then lets go out tonight for dinner and just get to know each other," she replied. They met again that evening at a restaurant of her choice as the table for two was set by a reservation she made. The young lady stopped him when he pulled his credit card and said, "A deed done without repayment is a reward unto itself." The following summer which happened to be a Saturday afternoon, they walked this time without a shopping cart. It was more crowded than usual when he kissed his new bride in an aisle remembered....

Where We Left Off...

A microphone hung inside the driver's side window as the music played. A title on the screen appeared "Rebel Without A Cause," introducing James Dean. It was a summer evening in the year of 1959 that we sat in my car and watched the drive-in movie. A waitress on roller skates knocked on the passenger side window and my girlfriend took the order of two cheeseburgers and fries with cokes and placed the tray on the seat between us. Some weeks later she moved to another state as her dad was transferred from his job to this new location. Our first love came and went in the blink of a calendar flipping its pages. She was someone who I wished remained with me for a possible future together. My college was also out of state and I moved there as well, leaving behind some memories which were never forgotten. In 1979 my car drove back to where it all started. Drive-in movies were a thing of the past just like payphones and tokens for the subway. A shopping mall now stood there but with the same out door parking lot. Maybe I fell asleep and started to dream as a microphone hung inside the driver's side window and the music played. Oldies music played from my car radio as a knock on the passenger side window woke me up. I looked at the tray in the middle of the front seat as an old girlfriend smiled back at me. It didn't matter what year it was anymore as we kissed once again. The girl on roller skates waved back at us and I could have sworn she had wings attached. On loves path a calendar flips for another chance as we continue where we left off....

A Picnic With Fireflies...

A blanket was spread on the grass just about the same time the sun went down. He took the bottle of wine from the cooler with ice and popped the cork as his glass was now full. Crickets began to chirp and fireflies blinked beneath the June sky. It was where he met his wife in this exact spot some forty years ago. She passed away from breast cancer six months into their marriage and he never really got over it, nor forgot the short time they spent together. His finger stirred the last ice cube in a glass of wine that melted on a blanket during a picnic with fireflies. One landed on the index finger of his left hand where his wedding ring still remained. He fell asleep and woke up as it was still the month of June, but forty years before. She took the bottle of wine from the cooler with ice and popped the cork as both their glasses were now full. He proposed to her that evening about the same time as the sun went down. Maybe little wings from another time were those of an angel who lit up another time around one summer evening. There was a second honeymoon during a picnic with fireflies....

Never Let Go...

Come back to the revolving door where we first missed each other. Then we can walk in the same direction once again. Now I can open a window that was once shut. This time never let go of my hand....

Life In The Fast Lane...

If the speed limit was 55, he would do 65. If the crosswalk sign said "don't walk," he would run across the street dodging traffic. Johnny would spend money faster than he could make it and racing motorcycles and skydiving were two big hobbies of his. It was life in the fast lane ever since he could remember. The dance club was crowded one Saturday evening as a silver ball spun and glittered from the ceiling above. He danced with all the hot ladies he could and bought them drinks with a credit card that soon would be expired. Jennifer stood at the bar and watched him dance in the fast lane. She was plain and simple in dress and definitely not his type she thought to herself. The last song was a slow one and Johnny noticed her staring at him from across the dance floor. She whispered in his ear while they danced and then he took her home. Something made him slow down when he found someone who cared and loved him for what he was. Maybe it was a halfway point of speed limits and crosswalks where we needed to take one step at a time. Johnny slowly put a ring on her finger as the next year they walked to the church instead of driving. Their wedding album was beautiful as I was the photographer who used to sky dive and race motorcycles with him. It's kind of strange how the name of the motel that they spent their honeymoon in was called "Life in the Fast Lane"....

Tara...

Tara was a baby rabbit that I named when my parents bought her at a local pet shop. She had long floppy ears typical of the Angola breed that she was had a beautiful combination of black and white fur from head to tail. One black ring surrounded her left eye and one white ring around her right eye. They were sky blue as if somehow human in nature. The cage sat on the terrace outside during the summer months and inside during the winter. I liked the winter months when she slept inside and jumped onto my bed and cuddled up next to me just like a human would do. Her little tongue would lick my face as if it was a kiss goodnight. Surprisingly she ate a lot of people food which most rabbits do not do. Tara loved my grilled cheese sandwiches which we often shared together for lunch. For thirteen years we grew up together until one summer afternoon she lay very still in the cage during the summer months on the terrace. A garden below the 25 floors I lived in was a small homemade grave where I had buried my beloved pet and friend. Eventually I moved out at 35 years old and got my own apartment. I put an ad in the paper for a housekeeper needed while at work during the day. The door bell rang and a young lady wearing black and white came in for the interview. Her ears seemed a little floppy and one black ring surrounded her left eye. The resume that was presented just had her first name, but that was all I needed. She asked me if I liked grilled cheese sandwiches and I smiled knowing that it was her. We find love in many ways in pets and humans and sometimes one becomes the other. I love you Tara....

A Backyard Of Dreams...

From the main floor of my parent's house were steps that led down to the basement. Walking to the right would lead to a door that opened into the backyard of dreams. It was a nickname I gave to this place where fond memories resided long after I had moved out. Growing up there was something to never be forgotten. I would play in the garden with some favorite toys as a child and as I got older I would mow the lawn and love the smell of the fresh cut grass during those summer months. There was a crank that would lower and raise the awning for shade as it also protected me from the rain and summer thunderstorms. To the right of this garden was the driveway where eventually I parked my first car before putting it in the indoor garage at the end of the path. A garden hose extended from inside the garage where every weekend I would proudly wash my blue 1969 Mustang. At 25 years old I moved out of the parents nest and got my own place. It is now 2007 and at 62 years old I decided it was time to buy a home of my own. I looked at houses for sale in a neighborhood that I grew up in many years before. It was on the same block, the same house, the same address. Down the basement steps I walked and to the right out the door to a backyard of dreams. I cut the grass which still smelled the same and cranked down an awning just before a summer thunderstorm. From the main floor of her parent's house just next to mine a long time ago was a girl who walked down some basement steps and into her backyard of dreams. At 60 years old she moved back to where she used to live. "I'll soap it up and you wash the car," she said. It was one weekend I totally forgot about but now remembered. My 1969 Mustang appeared in a driveway as she cranked down the awning just before a summer thunderstorm. Sometimes we sleep and wake up into a backyard of dreams....

A Salad Bar With Special Dressing...

Dinner was ordered at a resort while on vacation and there was time enough to go up to the self service salad bar. It was casual as the guests wore tee shirts and shorts and or jeans, except for me and the lady ahead of me on the line. I wore a shirt and tie and she had a beautiful red dress on. She filled a brown wooden bowl with plain green lettuce and then poured her favorite dressing on it, which happened to be mine also. At a table across from me she sat and looked up and smiled between bites as I did the same. We both got up and approached each other at the same and said "may I join you?" We laughed and sat down together and talked more than we ate. The same salad with the same dressing started our conversation and then the waitress brought out the main course dinner. Two dishes were placed in front of us as we each stared at the others, medium rare steaks with two baked potatoes. "How could this be, the same dinner also?" I said to her. "Looks like we have more in common than expected," she replied. Eventually we asked why the formal dress when everybody else was casual? Our answers were the same as we explained we wanted to meet that special someone. That was the most important part of this conversation as our eyes met with a special glow and a feeling that overwhelmed us. The waitress cleared our table carefully not to disturb our kissing over the table. The following summer we went back to this resort as a couple who were about to be married. The dining room was filled with guests in casual attire except for me and the bride. That's the way we planned it to be as she stood in front of me at the open salad bar. A salad bar with special dressing....

M.R. & G.W...

The summer after high school graduation they sat on their favorite beach together. Four years of being sweethearts since they first met back in their freshman year. I remember it as though it was yesterday and recall every detail of that July afternoon in the summer of 1961. We held and shared a seashell as the sound of the waves whispered in our ears. It also said "I love you forever" in our own minds. With a blue magic marker I wrote our initials M.R. & G.W. and then threw it back into the ocean. Gail then said "If I find it again, will you marry me?" "You've got a deal my darling." I replied. About 15 minutes later the lifeguard yelled from his post high up on a platform "Shark! Everybody out of the water, now!" That was the last time I saw my sweetheart alive. It is now 1981 on a hot July afternoon at a beach of memories I would rather forget. The sunset glistened on the incoming waves and I wasn't sure if it was a ghost or someone real. She looked the same as I remembered her to be and walked with a seashell in her hand held to her ear. My hand reached out to hers and I placed it to my ear with waves and "I love you forever" echoing in my heart. She pointed to the blue magic marker that once wrote a promise and said to me, " I found it again, now will you marry me?" It was an outdoor wedding on a beach that lasted from mid afternoon to sunset the following July. A huge banner was posted at the entrance of this ceremony which read M.R. & G.W....

Shall Forever Be...

You smile at the written words he wrote and feel them in your heart. I hold hands with you as we both know it is just a dream, yet we awake with a smile. A reality known by only the two of us. Such is a kiss and hug when you write back to me in words where our hearts shall forever be....

Round Trip Ticket...

She purchased a round trip ticket to visit from her state to his for two weeks. They had known each other online for about a year and also talked on the phone frequently. No motels or hotels, his place was where she was going to stay for better or for worse. He met her at the airport and for the first time a hug and kiss were shared in person. A candlelit table with a home made dinner set the mood with soft music in the background. She slept in the guest room and dreamed of the night before as so did he. Breakfast was prepared ahead of time as he knew what she liked and about what time she usually woke up. The two weeks flew by as each day was better than the next. He kept a surprise from her as being shy and not sure when to give it to her. The ride back to the airport was mostly silent as they both reflected on the past two weeks which were probably the best times of their lives. She walked up the ramp and turned around just before boarding the plane. He waved at her with tears running down his cheeks and she couldn't take it anymore. The airline attendant said "tickets please" as she held it up and ripped it in half. She ran back down the ramp into his open arms as they kissed and hugged for a second time. He opened a little black box and slipped a ring on her finger which was the surprise that it was supposed to be. The guest room was now empty as they both slept and awoke where couples usually do. Flights come and go between cities and states where people meet and leave. In this case love found a way on the floor of an airline terminal where we tear a ticket in half, which makes us whole....

A Flower For Jennifer...

It was at a summer day camp for kids where it all began. I was nine years old and Jenny was seven. We became close friends that summer and so did our parents as it was found out that we all lived in the same neighborhood back in Brooklyn. The summers were spent in the Catskill Mountains and our time was shared together in between trips from home to there. We sat in a field alone together the following summer and I plucked a small yellow dandelion and gave it to Jenny. At ten years old I didn't know what else to do to show my affection for her. The eight year old kissed me on the cheek and that made it official. We were now boyfriend and girlfriend. Both sets of parents enrolled us in the same high school some years later and then it happened again. I plucked a flower from the schools garden, a yellow tulip which I handed her during our freshman year. She kissed me on the cheek and we held hands as boyfriend and girlfriend once again. I pinned a beautiful carnation on her graduation dress and she kissed me on the lips for the first time. Our parents would often visit each other's homes with all of us together as a very close bond had been established. It was Valentines Day when I went to the store and bought a single red rose for my Jennifer. Both parents knew in their hearts that this was becoming a serious relationship. The college years came and went along with many flowers and kisses that would lead up to a final conclusion. That was a ring that Jennifer accepted for a proposal of marriage. It was an outdoor ceremony during the month of June at a resort in the Catskill Mountains we both grew up in where it all started. Before the priest blessed our marriage I bent down and plucked a small yellow dandelion from the field. It was a flower for Jennifer....

The Librarian...

He sat in the fiction section of the library which bought all three of his books. The librarian sat during her lunch hour at the same table as he while reading his second book "Where Angels Tread." She glanced at him and said "Hey, you're that author aren't you?" Michael nodded his head and smiled back at her. "Can I have your autograph please?" she asked. He took a pen out of his shirt pocket and signed it with a message that looked so familiar to her. "I feel like I've been through this before. You know; that déjà vu feeling?" He opened her book to a certain page with a certain title called "The Librarian..." "Look familiar?" he asked. "Yes, it was your best story from your first book," she replied. And so they dated for the next few months just like in the short story that was written about a year before. "On Loves Path" was his third book as he sat in the fiction section of the library. She sat at the same table and asked for his autograph as Michael smiled once again. "Have we met before?" she asked. He opened his third book to a certain page with a title that looked so familiar to her. "The Librarian..." We sit quietly in an aisle at a table where fiction and reality somehow become the same. If you don't believe me, then just ask the librarian....

The Portrait...

The portrait hung on a wall in the museum, of a young girl sitting by a window holding a flower in her hand. Outside the sunrise was seen in the background and in the room where she sat, a tear dripped down one cheek. Her deep blue eyes reflected the loneliness that was felt by the painter who did this masterpiece of emotion some thirty years ago. He walked into the gallery as the patrons flocked around him for an autograph. "Who was she and where is she now?" most of them asked, as he replied "A young 16 year old who had the face of an angel which I needed to paint a portrait of." "Where did the flower come from and why was she crying?" they asked. "It was a flower I gave to her before the painting began and she decided to hold it in her hand. Maybe the tear that she cried was from when I told her to keep it". He was 20 years old at the time he painted her, just four years older than she was. The 50 year old artist stood in front of the portrait long after the others had left and tried to wipe away a tear from her eye on the wall in front of him. She stood unnoticed in the crowd just from a little while ago and then tapped him on the shoulder. A 46 year lady held a similar flower in her hand and said "remember me?" A romance that happened some thirty years ago was reunited once again with two single tears dripping down each one of their cheeks. They sat together in front of a window for a wedding photographer's photo. The sun rose in the background as they each held a flower in their hand. You can go to the gallery and see it on the wall now in a museum of your choice. It still says "The Portrait"....

Darlene...

A sixteen year old runaway sat crouched in an alley just behind my house. Her hands reached out to a wired garbage can with burning newspapers that kept her warm this cold December night. I walked towards her slowly and asked how she was. The frightened and confused teen just cried. My warm coat was placed over her shoulders and I just held her for a moment until she started to talk to me. "Three years living on the streets and I'm tired now and just want to die," she said. "Well how about just for now you can stay with me over night and then decide the rest of life?" She agreed and held my hand as we walked together back to a home she maybe never had before. The young runaway stayed over longer than expected and even sat beneath my Xmas tree a week later. A necklace with her name was my gift to her as "Darlene" decided to stay here with me permanently. I never told her about a daughter lost some thirty years ago as a runaway but somehow I think she knew. On loves path we meet a stranger in the present that maybe we once knew in the past....

That Never Really Left...

Some things in our lives are taken away for better or for worse. A subway token replaced by a swipe metro card that sometimes wouldn't work. 25 cents a slice of pizza which we all miss with today's crazy prices. For me it used to be the drive in movies that I missed the most. My old neighborhood was still there but a shopping mall had replaced a special outdoor theater that used to be part of growing up. I rolled down my window and imagined the waitress on roller skates with a pony tail placing a tray of food for me and my girlfriend. We missed some of the movie back then as we hopped into the back seat and made out for a while, yet we managed to see the end of the film. A car parked next to mine and she got out to go to the mall. I felt that this lady was once here a long time ago and called out her name from a memory almost forgotten. She looked at me with familiar eyes and asked "do you remember when this place used to be a drive-in movie?" "Yes, I remember," I replied. "Can we sit for a few minutes together and talk?" she asked. "Please do," I said. There was a knock on my driver's side window as a girl on roller skates with a pony tail placed a tray of food. The old movie replayed itself as we sat in the back seat for a while but never missed the ending. On loves path there are lovebirds who pull into a parking lot that they never really left....

Remember Me...

Remember me? We were childhood sweethearts a long time ago in a place we no longer live. Email was exchanged plus phone calls later on which soon stopped. Maybe we can get together sometime in the future? He awoke from a dream as she slept through the night. Her hand held the phone as a number was dialed when she asked, "Remember me?"

The Sprinkler...

I turned the nozzle and magically the sprinkler came to life. It whirled around spinning the cold water on my parent's backyard lawn. Those were memories of hot summers gone by when I danced around the water and cooled off in my pre-teen years. Beth was a next door neighbor about my same age who often joined me as we played and giggled together. What made me think of her some forty years later, I don't know. I just did. It was time for me to move out of the apartment I was living in and buy my own house. An advertisement in the paper had me notice a house for sale in the old neighborhood I grew up in. It was the same exact address where my parents used to live. How freaky is that? The outside looked the same and of course the rooms inside were much different than what I remembered. In the backyard garden plants and grass and flowers decorated a memory of once was. Just one thing was missing, the sprinkler. It was early June when I moved in and immediately went to the store to pick up an item for my new backyard. My fingers turned the nozzle which made me feel like a kid again as the cold water whirled and spun about the backyard. I danced around in the hot summer sun but the sprinkler kept me cool. "Hello said my new neighbor, my name is Beth," she said from next door. My jaw dropped and was speechless for a few seconds until the reality of it hit me like a sledgehammer. We giggled together once again as that afternoon we played under the hot June sky. There was an outdoor wedding the following summer in my backyard and the guests were pleasantly cooled off when I turned on the nozzle that sprayed cold water from the sprinkler. On loves path we remember an event and even a name that brings us back to a location we once cherished. Such is the case of a childhood memory and a wife to be called Beth....

Forever Written...

The writer writes and the reader reads. He becomes part of the characters and feels their emotions as so does the reader. That is the connection that bonds the both of them. My pen sat in one hand as the other rang her doorbell. She answered as a signature was forever written in her heart....

Jennifer's Doll...

Jennifer's doll was kid friendly with squeezable parts that would talk to you. She came with batteries and 5 different outfits to dress her with. Her hair could be brushed and accessories like handbags, hats, shoes, and jewelry were included. Mom added a small dollhouse for her daughter to play with as this made Jennifer very happy on her seventh birthday. At 12 years old her mother got sick and had to go to the hospital as dad watched over the both of them. The little girl dressed up her friend in a nurse's uniform and brought it to the room where she and dad were visiting mom. It was kind of strange that the receptionist looked so much like Jennifer's doll. Her mother came home fully cured of the cancer that riddled her body for over a year as dad and his daughter welcomed her back. She was dressed in white with a similar hand bag, hat, shoes, and jewelry. It may have been important that the little girl named her old and new friend after her mom. Sometimes toys or make believe friends are really those who we love in their image. A healing plus a miracle, case in point on loves path by Jennifer's doll....

And So The Red Rose...

And so the red rose sprang from the fertile soil and grew its petals to a flower. Its fragrance was unique and unsurpassed in the essence of true love. Careful to be held for thorns may prick an unwary finger with intentions to deceive the recipient of this gift. It sat in my garden until the time needed to be given and received with gratitude. She held it to her nose and sniffed with delight as then it was placed in a vase of water. It became many a gift during our courtship and into our marriage through many a holiday and birthday. Finally it rested where she was at peace in our later years where loves cycle comes full circle. And so the red rose....

Parole Board...

Two prisoners were serving life sentences, one with the possibility of parole, the other with none. They became close friends from the very beginning and through the long years they thought of each other as brothers. At 68 years old, John told his buddy of the upcoming parole board meeting next week and said to Bill "wish me luck my friend, I want to walk and sit on a park bench outside of these walls and just feed the pigeons like I did once when I was a kid." Bill gave him a brotherly hug and said "good luck and I know you will be out of here soon." John told Bill the good news next week as he was free to live the rest of his life outside the walls that kept him confined for too long to remember. The guards opened the front prison gate as Bill escorted him until no further he was allowed. John collapsed in the summer heat from natural causes before his final freedom was obtained. John picked his lifeless up and held him tightly as he said "don't worry buddy, I'll get you there," with tears running down his cheeks. Nobody stopped him and as a matter of fact they followed Bill to a park bench where he laid his brother to sit down. He fed the pigeons that sat there and all was well with a dream that came true. On loves path a destination is reached where long time friends and brothers need to go. Bill was released on good behavior where the parole board was a judgment by God....

The Repairman...

Something surfaced in a conversation between my fiancé and I about how we met. She said to me, "The day before we got together I had a computer technician come over and fix it for me. If that didn't happen, we would have never met," she said. "Now that's really strange, I remember also having mine fixed the day before we met online," I replied. It happened to be that we both lived in the same neighborhood and we decided to check our records and bills of who came that particular day. The name of the serviceman was the same and went to each of our houses 3 hours apart. "You know Hun, I think we should try to contact this guy and thank him for what he has done." She agreed and we called up to find out that he still worked there. I told my story to him and how he was responsible for the future wife and I getting together. He said "I was supposed to be the best man at my daughters wedding but she was killed in an auto accident. I feel great now knowing that I have connected two other people with the same plans as she once had." My heart sank as what he had just said and with no hesitation I replied, "We need a best man at our wedding, will you honor us with that?" He said in a choked tearful voice, "I'll be there!" On loves path we have three people who needed to connect with other, each for their own personal reasons. Maybe that is why timing is everything for those needed to be there. I went to another home and repaired another computer....

Beth...

Beth was one of those runaways in a file of missing reports that was never solved. What makes this case interesting is what happened some ten years later in a park where she once played. Here is what happened... She disappeared in 1973 at the age of 15 as I reported it to the police. They told me they needed 24 hours before an investigation would be made, as most of them would come home before then. My daughter never came. Ten years later I walked through a borough I used to live in and sat on a park bench where we used to play together. A 25 year old sat down next to me and cried with something she was holding close to her chest. It was a small teddy bear that she took with her, a childhood friend that was given to her on her tenth birthday by me. Beth looked at me with familiar eyes and said "Is that you dad?" All I could do at that moment was hold her in my arms and share the same tears that she was pouring out. We drove back to where I now live as Beth apologized to her mom and dad and we all clutched a teddy bear that brought us back together again. No reports were given as to the return of the missing Beth. It wasn't a public concern you see, but a private matter in a case file which needed to be solved by just me and mom. On loves path we have here two parents in search of their missing daughter. Maybe a teddy bear or a park she used to play in had something to do with it. Whatever it was doesn't really matter. She stood over my shoulder as I wrote this story as a teddy bear secretly smiled in her bedroom that she now sleeps in once again....

When We Finally Hold Hands...

To touch without actually holding hands may come in the form of something that has been written. It brings us together not in miles but a closeness of the heart which it all matters from. So in our thoughts and dreams there is a connection to be made which one day can be felt when we finally hold hands....

The Right Thing To Do...

Next to a pole on a subway platform sat a red wallet. He bent down and picked it up just as the train was arriving. Credit cards, photos, a driver's license, and in a small zippered compartment was 700 dollars in cash. Maybe that was a Xmas bonus he thought to himself as this was the middle of December. He would carefully place each item back in its proper place that night when getting home from work. She noticed her wallet was missing on lunch hour that day when going shopping and cried all the way home. Esther looked through the peephole of her front door that evening when it rang at eight o'clock. She saw a hand holding a red wallet and immediately opened the door. "I found your wallet next to a pole on the subway platform and thought you may want it back," Michael said. She cried once more, but this time with tears of joy. "I never thought I would see it again, especially with all my credit cards and 700 dollars in cash," she said. "It was the right thing to do," Michael replied. They spent Xmas and New Years Eve together from a chance set of circumstances that don't usually happen in our lives. One year later on that same day, she picked up a black wallet that sat next to a pole on that same subway platform. The photo and name on his driver's license matched that of her boyfriend Michael. He opened the front door as they both stood there with a familiar set of events a year before. It all seemed to point to the right thing to do. He opened a special zipped compartment that an engagement ring was kept for a special occasion. Michael placed it on Esther's finger just before the train arrived. On loves path we find items lost and found in a place where we are supposed to be at the right time and the right place. After all, it's the right thing to do....

A Doll For All Seasons...

Mary Beth had a special doll who sat with her through all different holidays and events. You might say she had more outfits than even mom. It was the love for this doll and its companionship that made a special and personal bond between the two. Not uncommon with kids growing up with their favorite toys. Her name was Dolores and she was a doll for all seasons. Their friendship remained even as Mary Beth was now 14 years old, a time when most had forgotten about their dolls. While crossing the street one day to catch her school bus, Mary Beth wasn't paying attention to the red light against her as a car tried to stop from hitting her but didn't succeed. She awoke after some extensive surgery as the nurse came in with a clipboard and reviewed her recovery status. "You're going to be good as new and in a few days and you will be going back home," she said. "Before you leave make sure to check under your pillow for a surprise to my most favorite patient." Just as the nurse was leaving the phone rang in her private room and it was dad. "I'll see you in the morning my darling, is there anything you want me to bring you?" he asked. "Yes daddy, bring me my doll please," she replied. That following morning dad showed up and soon afterwards Mary Beth fell asleep with Dolores in her arms. Two days later it was time to leave the hospital as she had fully recovered. Just as she started to walk out of her room, Mary Beth turned around and remembered to look under her pillow for a surprise the nurse had promised her. She lifted the pillow to find a small name tag with the name Dolores. Dad picked up his daughters doll that she almost left behind and said "I've never seen this outfit on your doll, I wonder where she got this nurses uniform?" Sometimes on loves path we encounter something human and something not. Maybe love and friendship have a way of connecting the inanimate object with a real person. For Mary Beth she continues to have a doll for all seasons....

Curtain Call...

I was lucky enough to be seated in the second row of the concert hall where she performed, just another fan of a famous country singer who applauded and cheered like the rest of them. The last song was her first big hit from 5 years ago and the crowd went crazy. Roses flew from the audience and decorated the stage with love and admiration just in front of the closed curtain that she walked behind. My dream girl came out for an encore performance as she picked up at random one of the roses that littered the stage. It briefly passed under her nose and then she raised it in the air and said "Thank you all, let's go another twenty minutes." Being in the second row, maybe I got a view of the almost impossible. The rose had a card attached with my name and phone number as I thought about the odds against that. Twenty minutes later, after the curtain call, she walked off stage holding it still in her hand. It was two days later that my usually quiet phone rang and I picked up the receiver. "I saw you in the second row staring at the rose I held with a card attached. Was it you?" I stuttered a few times before the word "yes" came out of my mouth. "You caught my attention even before that and I would like to meet you in person," she said. Her chauffeur picked me up and drove to a house that most only see in dreams and magazines. No glitter with fancy clothes, just a plain girl in jeans and a tee shirt who offered me a beer and not champagne. We had much in common which is unlikely in the difference of our status and lifestyle. It was six months later that I ended up moving in with her as loneliness and the need for love knows not the rich nor the poor. The band took a break at our wedding after I asked and sat in for the drummer when I played our wedding song. My wife smiled and threw a rose as I did an encore performance via the curtain call. On loves path we sit in a row and stand on a stage where roses are thrown and sometimes accepted. Case in point where two people pull the strings on a curtain call....

The Suitcase...

Nancy was about to leave her small basement apartment for a long awaited three day visit to someone special she met online. The suitcase was packed and put in the back seat of a taxi cab that drove her to the airport. They already knew what the other looked like from photos sent through email and even talked quite frequently on the phone for the six months they had known each other. The states weren't that far away as the plane ride took only forty five minutes. Michael stood and watched the arrival board as the flight came in on time. She walked down the ramp and he greeted her with a red rose and a kiss on the cheek. It was the perfect beginning for a three day holiday weekend to start off with. Nancy was to sleep in the guest bedroom of his condo where his grown son had left some years before. Status of the two was now similar as both were divorced from previous marriages. He placed the rose in a vase and sat it on her night table which would stay there for three days and nights. Time had a way of slowing down for them and it actually felt like they had been together for a whole week. He was a perfect gentleman and made no unwanted advances that would jeopardize their first live meeting together. The time came when she had to catch a flight back to where she lived. Michael drove Nancy to the airport with a fresh red rose to establish that his love for her was the same as when they had met. She smiled at the departure gate and they both had a few moments where a passionate kiss was exchanged. He picked up the suitcase that she was going to take aboard and said "this feels way too light, did you forget things to pack?" Nancy replied "no, it's actually empty." Michael then knew something that she had in mind all along. They held hands in the front seat of his car on the way back to his condo. A guest room was no longer needed as the two slept together in the master bedroom. On loves path a three day stay becomes one of permanence. You might say one really never wanted to leave in the first place, and the other always wanted her to stay from the beginning. A meeting of the minds and hearts of those who look inside the suitcase....

How Far...

How far to reach out when a thought is right next to us. So let us travel in a dream where we meet without transportation. Who is to say where our reality or fantasy begins and ends? Not me you see, for I have known you all my life....

Cheers...

On the other side of the square shaped bar she sat, stirring a martini with a stirrer and a look of daydreaming in her eyes. About fifteen feet away he sat just opposite her doing the same with his Bloody Mary. Robert looked up at the same time as Helen and each looked at one another as both raised their drinks which in an unspoken language meant "Cheers." He had the bartender buy her the next one and she smiled from across the other side. Helen got up and walked around to his side of the bar and asked if she could sit on the empty stool next to his. They clicked glasses the next few rounds before closing as the bartender joined in with "This one is on me," as he said "Cheers." The daydreaming and the loneliness took on a new and sudden joy of being happy once again. In two more hours it would be New Years Eve and Robert would be sitting in Helen's living room as she invited him over to stay. A lot was spoken that night and felt as the two hugged just before the ball came down. They stirred each others glass with a finger and mind and heart that was no longer in a daydream. A whisper could be heard just before they fell asleep on the same pillow. "Cheers." On loves path it may be across a square of fifteen feet or so where two eyes meet and decide not to be alone anymore. Case in point where Robert and Helen heard the clapping of hands at their wedding where glasses clicked together and voices echoed the sound of "Cheers"....

Where Or When...

Where or when the two shall meet has less importance than who we are meeting with. For you there is no distance too far, no place that cannot be found. You see we have already met in a dream, and that alone has brought us together. Look not behind you but just ahead and in front with outstretched arms....

A Flower For Florence...

It took a little longer for Florence to get to the podium where the microphone was waiting. Her wheelchair moved slower than most walking legs do. It was an uplifting speech for the girl who graduated her class with top honors and achievements that most of us never attain. I was her English professor and wheeled her onto the stage that day of her graduation. She was a beautiful young lady who spoke with words that I would have never dreamed of. My guess is that whatever God takes away in our physical abilities is made up for in another special sense that overcome that obstacle. It wasn't by chance that at her next graduation from college I pushed the wheelchair to the podium just as I did in high school. She asked me to you see, and I said yes. Two announcements were made as I handed a flower for Florence as we both spoke into the microphone. The first asked her to marry me, the second said yes. She stood up out of her wheelchair and walked for the first time in her life. Why or how? We may never know. Just before I slipped the ring on her finger at our wedding vows, there was a flower for Florence. On loves path age not needs to be a number, nor whether we walk or sit as the podium with a microphone awaits. Such is the case in point with a flower for Florence....

As We Slept That Night...

Every summer I think back and remember something that once took place. It happened on a late July afternoon back in 1968 at my uncle's hotel in the Catskill Mountains. At that time I was 21 years old and the girl I had met that summer just turned 20. We hit it off right from the beginning and for the two months that year we were inseparable. You might say it was a first love that is always remembered no matter what year it is. The last moment of our time together was a mountain climb that took about an hour and a half to reach the top. A boulder we climbed and sat on provided a fantastic view of the green countryside below us. We held hands and kissed until there was nothing left but a full moon and stars which covered us as we slept that night. If nothing else, then I had to go back there just for the view. My 1988 Ford Mustang made the trip as I checked into a place which was no longer my uncle's hotel, but still there anyway. It was my now 41 year old legs that climbed that mountain which took a little longer than before. A 40 year old lady held her hand out on the top of a boulder that she remembered and had to return to also. We kissed and held hands until there was nothing left but a full moon and stars which covered us as we slept that night. On loves path we take a boulder and climb it for a view once seen before. Fresh legs with a memory that only love can restore as we slept that night....

Was Always Saved...

On the rebound we find sometimes someone who should have been there in the first place. Grass is greener on the other side until fall leaves reveal true colors of those across the yard. My first garden tomato, my first planted rose, was always saved for you....

The Rest Should Take Care Of Itself...

The writer checked his replies from a well known web site where his stories were posted. One was dated August seventh and it read "you're writings are like a lyrical dance." Her photo was as attractive as the written reply which he often looked at before. It was the kind of compliment that touched him deeply and so the writer sat down and decided to create a story just for her. Here is that story... Somewhere between the distances of where they each lived, was a vacation resort that he went to for the first time. The writer sat at the bar inside the outdoor pool area and sipped on cold beer under a roof that kept the hot July summer sun away. He wasn't thinking about stories or web sites, just enjoying a nice 3 day weekend. A blonde lady just sat down on the other side of the bar and she was the one whose photo he often looked at with a special reply attached. Carrie looked at him at the same time and saw the writers face by heart from all the stories she had read with his photo attached. They sat together as meeting for the first time was quite an unexpected thrill neither ever thought would happen. She opened her bag and took out two of his books that she was now reading for the second time and Michael autographed both. He had brought some extra copies of his third book "On Loves Path," just in case. He gave it to her and said, "This one's on me." Over the remaining two days and nights there were some kisses and hugs exchanged somewhere between the distances of where they each lived. This story doesn't have an ending for it hasn't happened yet, but maybe soon. On loves path we don't need an ending necessarily, just a beginning and a middle. The rest should take care of itself....

The Following Round Trip...

The loneliness in itself has its own purpose, for that time sits next to us the peace and solitude needed to reflect and ponder. With that the next day our heart rides a train where each stop people get on and off, some remembered and some not. The final destination is not our goal, but the enjoyment of the journey getting there. You put down the newspaper and I put down my book, for then we had time to read each others eyes. Two seats reserved on the following round trip....

Grandma...

My name is Arlene and here is my story... It started back in 1956 when I was seven years old. This was a Christmas Eve where grandma held me on her lap and pointed out the window as I watched the snow blanket the ground outside. Music played from mom and dad's radio with songs that fit the occasion of the evening. Red and blue and green lights twinkled on the pine tree that sat in our living room as it was now time to open our presents. Grandma smiled as I tore the wrapping paper from the small box beneath that awaited my eager hands. My first doll it was that grandma had given me and little Betsy became my new friend. I hugged her and then grandma as she kissed me goodnight and tucked me in as the radio played "Silent Night". In 1966 when I was seventeen, grandma passed away. The following Christmas Eves were not the same as I missed sitting on her lap and opening presents. Another ten years flew by and at 27 I was already married and had a daughter of my own. She pointed out the window and was excited to see the snow blanket the ground outside. The next morning she came and woke me up and said, "Mommy, there is still one present under the tree that wasn't opened yet." I was sure there nothing left but I looked anyway to make her happy. Why the tree lights were still on confused me, for I turned them off the night before. A small box sat there as my daughter handed it to me and said, "Unwrap it mommy". I tore the paper off and there was a doll I used to play with. A small tag was attached that read "made in the U.S.A. 1956". On loves path we think back and remember. Then we find that it never really left us. I sat on her lap as she pointed out the window as the snow blanketed the ground. The red and blue and green lights twinkled on the pine tree as a song called Silent Night played on my stereo. Thank you grandma....

For Adults Only...

It was a place to go back to just for the fun it, an amusement park for kids and adults which sits on a map in Brooklyn, NY, known as Coney Island. From where I now lived it was an hour and thirty minutes away, so there I headed with a full tank of gas and a kids' smile on an adult face. Nathan's hot dogs and fries was the first stop and they still tasted just as good as twenty five years ago. The same rides and attractions were still there and I felt like the past had come to life once again. The tunnel of love was a ride where the cars were set up to fit two people. Dark rooms became lit up with romantic scenery and music and I suddenly remembered someone who sat next to me back then, a childhood sweetheart who I wondered about where she is now. I gave the man my ticket for the ride and sat in the last car alone, with my arm around an image from the past. We giggled and kissed until the ride was over as kids often do. The adult next to me held my hand as we exited the ride and said "I'm glad you were here again." On loves path we take a trip back to a place we had fun as kids. Then another joins in with the same intentions as you. A childhood dream for adults only....

Never Locked Again...

Beyond the daily routine is a window not made of glass, but of someone looking in. It comes in the form of another trying to enter a door which is now locked. For the first time she opened it and saw something of a dream she once had. He wiped his feet on the welcome mat and entered her heart, a window not made of glass, but a door she never locked again....

Maria's World...

Maria's world was like a silent movie, pictures without sound as she was born deaf. Yet one afternoon there was a voice to be heard that forever changed her life. This is her story... The light was green to cross the street, a visual thing of safety that she did a million times before. A man on the other side of the crosswalk looked to his left and saw a speeding car chased by the police with sirens blaring. She heard a voice in her head saying "Lookout, lookout!" which the man shouted some distance away. Her instincts had her jump back to the curb but she tripped and fell when her head hit the pavement. Maria rode in an ambulance where the stranger sat next to her on the way to the emergency room. A mild concussion with a few bruises was better than being dead. The man who saved her life was there when she woke up and felt him holding her hand. Their eyes communicated with nothing else to be said or done. It was maybe a year later that she heard wedding bells for the first time. Why was her hearing restored, the doctors had no answer for it. All I know is that I published this story in the human interest column of my newspaper back in 1975. She went on to write a book which became a bestseller; it was called "Maria's World." On loves path we find a stranger at the right place and time. Compassion and caring for another has a miracle where the one less of her five senses are restored. I am glad to be her husband and part of Maria's world....

Jerry's Car Service...

Two total strangers sat a few stools away from each other where most drown their loneliness with unseen tears. Nancy got change from her last twenty dollar bill and then tipped the bartender as she said goodnight. George did the same and both ended up a block away walking into the car service that would take them home. The dispatcher announced that the next car was available as both stood up at the same time waiting for their ride. George said "if it is alright with you, maybe we can share this ride so the other doesn't have to wait for another car." "He can drop you off first, then me afterward." Nancy agreed and they both sat in the back seat as she told her address to the driver. George couldn't believe his ears as she told the driver of the exact same address where he lived also. It was an apartment building, just on a different floor. "Looks like we're going to the same place," Nancy said. The huge tip to the driver was on George as he suddenly felt that this was a meeting destined to happen. Each pressed the elevator button and then looked at the other like the evening had just begun. "I'm hungry, want to ride up one more floor and I'll fix us both something to eat?" George replied "yes, thank you for asking." There were no more unseen tears of loneliness as a short three months later he moved in with her. The following summer they drove to the rented hall where they were to be married. George made a special phone call to a special place that changed their lives around. They sat in the back seat of a car that would take them on their honeymoon. He was glad to save the business card of "Jerry's Car Service." On loves path we made a few stops to get there. A lonely bar, a car service, and finally home....

Meatballs And Spaghetti...

There were maybe 5 or 6 close friends who joined me for my seventh birthday party. Mom and dad fixed meatballs and spaghetti, a favorite that we all loved to eat. A funny moment happened when Jill who was sitting next to me slurped up a few strands as the red sauce hit her directly on the nose. I licked it off and both of us along with the rest of my friends laughed out loud. In a way, maybe it was actually a first kiss. That particular meal remained my favorite along with some fond memories of that seventh birthday party. Twenty something years later I went to my favorite restaurant for a birthday to be celebrated by myself. A lady sat down and ordered the same dish as I did in the booth just in front of me. I thought nothing of it until she slurped up a few strands as the red sauce hit her directly on the nose. "Jill, is that you?" I asked. She smiled with the same look as before and said "yes, it's me." There was a second kiss this time around after licking the sauce off of her nose as we both laughed out loud. There was a menu at our wedding reception with the usual except for the main course. It can be seen on the bride and grooms faces as slurping up a few strands with red sauce in a main dish called meatballs and spaghetti. On loves path we take a favorite childhood dish and carry it over to adulthood. Then we share a table for two in a restaurant where both are about to meet again. Main courses served up with meatballs and spaghetti....

For The Love Of Rose...

Watch me bloom and smell my fragrance. Soft pink or deep red, each with romantic intentions. Stand me up in a vase or plant me in a garden, for I am yours always. Cellophane holds and wraps me gently by myself as given to another of your love shown. A dozen of me on Valentines Day. He held me gently and passed me on for the love of rose....

A Folder Called "My Pictures"...

Old photos of those throughout the years sit in a folder called "my pictures." All of them were once people that I could have possibly met but never did. Some exchanged phone calls besides chat and email as plans to meet always failed. The excuses ranged from being too busy now, too far away, or I met someone else. This folder had to be deleted in order to stop reflecting back to what could have been. The phone sat quiet and still, the doorbell never rang, and no new pictures were ever sent. Hello and goodbye were all too close together for anyone to bear. She looked through her folder called "my pictures" as looking back on people she could have met. A phone number was etched in her memory that somehow was never forgotten. I answered the call and she said "you've got mail." It was a new photo of someone that still never left my heart. We finally met when she realized there were no more excuses to give. And so we now click on the same computer and look at our wedding album in a folder called "my pictures". On loves path the deleted go to the recycle bin, yet are never forgotten in ones heart....

Essence Of Love...

The essence of love is to give and not receive. It expects nothing in return and therefore is unconditional. It holds friendship and lovers together with the same purpose. It is between man and woman as well as nature and all living things....

G H And J B...

The home had its usual variety of senior citizens where a game of checkers or cards passed the time. For Gregory Hanson it was daydreaming about the past. The 93 year old would stare at the T V in the lobby but not really see what was on. Next to him sat Julia Barnes, a 90 year old who did the same. They talked for a few minutes before the nurses gave them their nightly medication to help them sleep. One day they decided to play a few games of checkers and get to know each other better. He noticed a ring on her finger that he saw in his daily daydreams and said "where did you get that?" She replied "from an old boyfriend in high school." He asked if he could look at more closely and she took it off her finger and handed it to him. Tears fell down the old mans cheeks as the initials inside the ring read "G H and J B forever." She read it once again and remembered as they both wiped each others tears and smiled. They held hands in front of a T V the next day but didn't really pay attention to what was on. That night Gregory and Julia took their pill but never swallowed it. Other plans were made to take a walk outside and leave. They found themselves in a 1963 Corvette convertible as he put an engraved ring on her finger just after graduation. There are no records of Gregory Hanson or Julia Barnes staying at a home for senior citizens, and so why not? No reason necessary you see. On loves path we take a memory and catch up with it in the future. Then to return for a second time where love needs to be....

In A Moment Captures...

To make love in a moment captures all time there afterwards. It is a plug that shall never be pulled from its socket. We then hold hands in dreams and in reality whether 500 miles away or 5 inches. My calendar is filled with you as yours is with me. In a moment captures....

The Merger...

Judy had to relocate to another city due to a merger with another company. So did another girl with the same name, only spelled differently, Judi. Neither one knew of the other but in a few short weeks when the move would take place, their lives would soon be dramatically changed. After getting settled into their new location and place of work, it was then that the miracle happened. It took place in the ladies room during a lunch break that both had at the same time. Judy was fixing her makeup in the mirror when the girl behind her stopped and starred in amazement and shock. Was it a reflection, a mirage, was she seeing double? An exact likeness of the girl behind her had them talk together as Judy and Judi met for the first time. It turned out they were identical twins separated at birth by adoption. How it was that both had the same name given just with a different spelling was strange enough, yet the same profession as a writer for a newspaper that would merge with another? They held each other and cried so many tears of joy that the previous 25 years had missed. The chief editor approved the story co-written by the twins and made front page headlines. "Identical Twins Reunite Due To A Merger." On love path we travel about 25 years to find a missing sister in another city. An unlikely place for a miracle to happen occurs in the ladies room where a special merger takes place....

Shall Be No More...

The empty vase shall be no more, for now sits a long stemmed rose. A phone once quiet will ring and there my voice will be heard. Your pillow now has a dream that was vacant for too long. You open the front door and I wipe my tired feet on a welcome mat that was forgotten too many times by the both of us. One hug, one kiss surrounds us without words needed to be said. It is then that loneliness shall be no more....

That Lies Within...

Jennifer had her hair done at the beauty parlor and then went home to apply some makeup. She was all decked out with bright red lipstick, eyeliner, rouge, and everything else possible for her night out. The guys wore their best clothes and favorite cologne as the games began to see who would meet who. Smiling white teeth with false words of other attentions were on the minds of the guys. When the one she met put his hand on her knee on a ride offered home, a red flag went up and she got out of his car and called a car service. She walked outside the following morning to the front of her house where the mailbox sat. The mailman made his usual delivery as she stood there without her hair done and no makeup. He handed her a dozen roses and said "this is not from another, but from me. You are the most beautiful lady I have ever seen and I hope you would accept this gift as a way of saying hello to you." She accepted with quite a surprise of being noticed without her makeup on. They dated soon afterwards without the best clothes and makeup and cologne and bright white teeth. Jennifer fell in love and no longer needed the things that would enhance the beauty that was already there. On loves path the complicated becomes the simple. What we put on or wear need not disturb the beauty that lies within....

When We Both Sleep...

The miles or states that separate us are just on a map of geography. On a pillow of my dreams and in my heart you are always next to me. If we awake with a smile then we have met before. Open your front door and let me in while I knock when we both sleep....

Johnny And Janet...

Johnny was just released from prison after serving 23 years for a manslaughter charge. He replayed the events in his mind about the struggle with his gun as it went off and fatally shot the store owner. It was never his intention to harm him during the botched robbery attempt. The look of hatred in the courtroom of the victim's daughter haunted him all that time as he cried for forgiveness in a cell that never heard him. All he wanted to do now was make peace with the store owner's daughter and alleviate the pain in his tortured soul. Johnny stood outside her door in a suit and tie, with some flowers in his hand and knocked on the now 46 year old daughter's home. Some years earlier dad came to her in a dream and told her he was alright now and happy in another place where we go, known as heaven. "Forgive the man who took me away, it was not his intention to do so." Janet opened the door and stood face to face without hate in her eyes, but forgiveness. His price was paid for the crime in those 23 years, yet he needed something more, a word of forgiveness. She read his tears and took the flowers from his nervous shaking hand. Dad whispered in her ear "thank you my darling Janet." Sometimes on loves path it's not about getting married, but simply forgiving and saving a tortured soul that needs to find peace with himself and with God. Case in point, Johnny and Janet....

Uncle Jim...

Uncle Jim was always there for me when I needed him. You might say he was like a second dad and friend at the same time. My name is Terry and I am now 53 years old and here is my story... He surprised me with a beautiful doll one Xmas Eve at the age of 7. When dad wasn't home sometimes on the weekend he would come over and help me ride my new bicycle. He often helped me with homework from school when my parents didn't know the answers. That was my uncle Jim, a kind and loving person who always thought about another and not himself. Mom and dad left me alone for the first time one summer weekend when I was 23 as they trusted my taking care of myself. The outdoor pool looked inviting as it was a hot July summer day. Uncle Jim sat home watching T V when suddenly he felt an extreme urge to check up on me. He drove faster than usual the ten miles that separated us with a sense of urgency. My leg cramped up in the deep part of the pool and I struggled to stay above the water to breath. All I could see was the sun above the bubbles of the surface when my lungs filled with water and I lost consciousness. The pressure on my back from his hands made me spit up the water that filled my lungs. Then his mouth blew into mine as my body revived itself. Uncle Jim has long since passed away but this is why I am still alive today. I thank him every day and night in a prayer to God. One Xmas morning I got up and proceeded to take down the tree. There was a doll there that wasn't there the night before. He let me know he still cared. That was my uncle Jim. On loves path we have a sense of urgency to check up and then save another ones life. A hunch, an intuition? Whatever it is doesn't matter. That is my story and I hope you all have someone with the love of Uncle Jim....

Sandy's Toy Chest...

Sandy's toy chest was a small 3 feet by 2 feet box with a lid that contained her favorite toys and possessions. It was something that a lot of children grow up with in their early years and usually brings back fond memories. She never really cared for being surprised and would rather know ahead of time any gift or present that mom or dad would give her. One day before her tenth birthday, dad told his daughter about her first wrist watch she was soon to receive. It was a Mickey Mouse watch which at that time was very popular amongst kids. Before her birthday the next day, dad passed away from a sudden heart attack as mom and daughter cried and mourned over the following months and years. Sandy grew up and became a twenty five year old ready to move out and live on her own. Mom suggested having her daughter look through any old toys or favorite possessions from that dusty old toy chest and throw out or take whatever she wanted. Sandy placed a garbage bag next to the chest and proceeded to throw out most of her fond memories. It was almost empty now except for a Mickey Mouse watch that seemed brand new, yet had a date with a message inscribed from a year of her tenth birthday. It read "happy birthday my darling Sandy". She put on her wrist as Mickey smiled and the second hand never stopped ticking. On loves path we find a gift sometimes that was supposed to be received, no matter how long it takes. Dad kept his promise to his daughter which this time she didn't know ahead of time. A surprise of love and knowing that he is still with her. Left forever in Sandy's toy chest....

Betty The Butterfly...

There were only about 2 hours of daylight left and I figured it's time to get out of this wooded forest before I got lost. It was a pleasant experience being alone with nature, yet one had to find his way back to the real world eventually. I pulled a broken compass from my pocket as now there was no direction to follow. The last 2 hours of daylight was spent going in circles as the meaning of being lost took on a sudden panic in my soul. If I could survive the night, maybe my last chance to get back home would be in the morning. Beneath the full moon that lit the forest came something that never was seen before at night. It was a butterfly, a creature of the day and not of the evening. She fluttered around me and then slowly moved in a direction that made me feel the need to follow her. 30 minutes later I spotted my car which was closer than I thought. She landed on my shoulder and I felt a kiss. I waved goodbye and thanked who I nicknamed Betty the Butterfly. Nobody would believe my story, so therefore I never told how I got out of being lost that night to anyone. The need for a pet had me drive to that store with a wide variety to choose from. It was that evening in the store when a butterfly landed on my shoulder as the owner never saw it, only me. "Never mind, I think I found my pet and possibly my guardian angel." The owner scratched his head and just said goodnight as I walked out the door. She flutters around my house now as nobody knows except you and me. If you ever feel lost at one time or another, just call out for Betty the Butterfly....

To Begin With...

No response necessary, for it has been read and felt. It can be seen in a dream of mine where you smile on a pillow not too far away. Such is the connection that we share until we meet. She opened the door one day to a dream and let him in. The pillow wasn't that far away to begin with....

A Name And A Scent...

The dream didn't take that long by our clocks standards, but for Ralph it seemed like a whole week. He basically met and dated someone who had the same romantic intentions of getting serious. No fooling around, no games, just a simple commitment to each other that is not very easy to find. The surroundings in his dream and even her face faded as most dreams do upon awakening, yet one thing stayed with him. The scent of her perfume remained and that alone made Ralph wonder about the reality of his dream. He had to go to a department store and try to identify if this scent really existed. The girl behind the counter said "you look so familiar to me, but I know you have never been in this part of the store before." Ralph was about to ask for samples to sniff when she leaned forward over the counter and the scent she wore was exactly the same as in his dream. "This may sound strange, but is your name Ralph? I had a dream about us as everything else faded except for your name." "When I smelled the scent on you, my dream then became as real as yours," he replied. They dated that night after she left work as now in reality there again were the same romantic intentions of getting serious. No fooling around, no games, just a simple commitment to each other that is not very easy to find. On loves path we have Ralph and a store clerk. Each with separate but similar dreams where some parts are faded and others remain while they are awake. A name and a scent....

Ahead Of Time...

Debbie packed her suitcase after staying for a pleasant 3 day weekend holiday. It was someone she met on the computer from another city and it felt for both of them like it lasted a whole week. Richard was basically shy and so he had a surprise planned ahead of time for her which he didn't want to give in person. It was planted in her suitcase the night before she left. It turned up in a blouse pocket that he bought her the Xmas before. Debbie was totally surprised at the engagement ring found there and she was doubly shocked to open her door and see him standing there. "I booked the same flight on your ride home and sat behind you without you noticing me. There was something I had to ask you in person," he said. Debbie was wearing her favorite blouse at the time and took the ring out of her pocket. "Put it on my finger Richard, you sweet loving man and don't say another word." His eyes filled with tears as so did hers and a kiss sealed an answer he need not ask now. On loves path we have a shy person who takes the extra step on a 3 day holiday weekend. A return flight has both on board where his question and her answer were tucked away ahead of time....

First Book Signing Event...

His first book signing event was set up and scheduled all by himself. It would take place at a resort he had been to last year where his first book was bought by many of the guests including even the owners. Both he and they agreed it would benefit his sales of the second book and attract old and new guests this upcoming Labor Day weekend. Michael remembered the compliments about the oldies music he played at the outdoor pool from his tapes and packed them once again. It was just before noon that his radio was set with the first tape of oldies as a display poster was set up in that pool area where his first book was sold. "Book Signing Today, Where Angels Tread, by Michael Reisman." The table in front of him had 50 copies as familiar guests from last year who had bought his first book stood on line for the second one. The bartender at the outdoor pool put in the next tape of oldies as half of the books were now sold. There were new guests that came from word of mouth about this event and in less than 3 hours all 50 copies were sold. Michael kept one for himself just in case he needed to show it to somebody else, for one day was left to stay at the resort. Sunday night he sat at the indoor bar as the first customer who bought his first book last year sat beside him. "Hey, remember me? My name is Sara." "Yes I do, my very first customer," he replied. They hugged and kissed as if it was supposed to happen this Labor Day weekend. He showed the second book he had written and autographed it just like he did the first one a year ago. She opened to a special page of his first book "Incredible Short Stories" and read the last paragraph. It described how two people would meet again and fall in love at a book signing event one Labor Day weekend. That is what happened exactly as a wedding soon followed. On loves path we have a writer and a devoted fan. Maybe one of his stories was an idea of events yet to happen, a wish? A desire? A premonition? In the end it doesn't really matter. I packed my car and traveled to a resort for my first book signing event....

Grandma's Chocolate Chip Cookies...

Marie was very close with her grandma and every visit was precious and special. Her most fond memories were of those special baked chocolate chip cookies with an aroma never to be forgotten. It still is now her favorite snack at the age of 30 when most adults forgot about what they grew up with. Marie moved out of mom's house to find an apartment of her own as she unpacked her belongings both necessary and personal. She just remembered a large sugar canister that she filled up the day before and needed it for her morning coffee. The drive back to mom's house was only fifteen minutes away, so Marie made the trip. Her mother stood there with the canister in her hand as if she already knew what her daughter had forgotten. "Bye mom, I'll see you next weekend," she said. Marie placed the full sugar canister on the kitchen counter for the next morning to be ready for her morning coffee. At 9 a.m. the next morning the coffee brewed and was finally ready. The sugar canister seemed to look a lot older and had a different design on it. Marie picked it up and it was extremely light considering it was once full with sugar. Suddenly the kitchen filled with an aroma of baked chocolate chip cookies. She opened the lid to find a piece of handwritten paper from another time that described grandma's secret recipe. They both sat together at the kitchen table and chatted about old times. Marie thanked her grandma for a precious and special visit. She sat quietly at the kitchen table and sipped on her coffee along with grandmas chocolate chip cookies. On loves path we take a memory and a canister of what was supposed to be sugar. Then we blend it with love and a visit from those who so touched our lives before. My name is Marie, would you like to come in and try grandma's chocolate chip cookies?

All Of Humanity...

I need not reach the multitudes and the numbers who read my writings. If there is only one fan then let that be my inspiration. It is not the sales nor the royalties, or the fame or fortune. To touch only one heart is a universal gift that is well received. Therefore I have reached all of humanity....

What We Are Looking For...

Veronica wheeled herself around the deck of the cruise ship and took in the sights with a smile on her face. She was bound to a wheelchair since being hit by a car at the age of seven and paralyzed from the waist down. The now twenty five year old decided it was time to meet someone and possibly get married. George introduced himself and the two played some shuffleboard as both seemed to hit it off right from the beginning. He wheeled her around for the next couple of weeks and they became inseparable for the rest of the cruise. George bent down a little and held her hands as they danced together with him on his feet and her on a wheelchair that spun around. Others noticed something special about them and often applauded their every move. Reservations were made the following summer on that same cruise ship as Veronica and George had plans to be married on the deck where they first met. Here is where something that couldn't be explained had happened. During the wedding ceremony the captain asked the bride if she took this man to be her husband. Veronica stood up and walked out of the wheelchair and said "yes, I do." On loves path we take a couple where one who used to just sit, now stands. A miracle of sorts which needs no explanation. Maybe true love in itself has the answer. For now, let the cruise ship hold and board others who need to find what we are looking for....

Party Balloons...

My eleventh birthday was very special and here is how I remembered it... The guests arrived from my invitations at school and mom and dad's phone calls to certain neighbors with kids my own age. There was a late guest that arrived as mom and dad said "Angela, a new boy on the block had just arrived and we think you should see what he came in with." In his hand he held a string and above his head floated a multi colored display of party balloons. He showed me a trick where if you rub them on your hair, a static is caused and you make them stick to the walls. His name was Billy, the new boy on the block. It was something from him that made my eleventh birthday very special. Ten years later I would find out how special it really was. My lunch hour came and in the office at now twenty one my co-workers surprised me with a birthday cake. A new employee came from another floor as he held a string and above his head floated a multi-colored display of party balloons. "Hello, my name is Billy," he said with a smile. Five years later it was my twenty sixth birthday and also my wedding day. Billy and I rubbed some balloons on our hair and stuck them to the walls throughout the hall. On loves path we have a guest who surprised a little girl on her eleventh birthday. He found her again when she turned twenty one and that was all that was needed to let a first love lead to a second time. A special memory for Angela and recorded in her wedding album where you can see on the walls some multi-colored party balloons....

Sights And Sounds...

She was lovely beyond words, so nothing was said. He was caring and thoughtful even though she never heard him say it. Beauty and love surrounded both while holding hands followed by a silent kiss. A world which often we do not see nor hear. He pets the dog and the three of them walk together, sights and sounds wrapped only unto what each could understand. There is no ugly when one is blind and no need to hear compassion and love when the other is deaf. Another sense takes control, maybe a flower given that was not seen by him, but smelt by her. A dog at the other end of a handle held, walks in front. The other holds her hand which she needs not to be heard. He was blind and she was deaf, yet he felt her written poem and she heard his whisper of how much he loved her. A title for those who can see and hear, "Sights and Sounds"....

Ruby Jones...

Ruby Jones was a piano player who sang the blues at a club in Chicago back in the 1940's. There she sat and sipped on scotch on the rocks between songs until I told her she had enough to drink. Ice water sat on the piano during her last set thanks to me, her manager, friend, and often lover in between, a white guy not often seen together with a black woman in those days. Ruby Jones had a drug habit which I wasn't aware of and that along with the scotch finally took her life at 32 years old. It was now in the 1970's when I moved back to Chicago and restored a club that had once been torn down. Outside was a neon sign that read "Ruby Jones Place." Nobody remembered her voice or the piano she once sat behind except me. A young lady came in and said she sang the blues and I auditioned her for a performance that would eventually sell out the next weekend. A glass of ice water sat on top of the piano as an old syringe needle lay in a waste basket long forgotten. I'm sure my calendar had the right date on it as read 1942. The wedding ring had a familiar name engraved inside. It was Ruby Jones....

Fortune Cookie...

A regular weekly trip on a Sunday afternoon was his way of satisfying the urge for Chinese food. He was a lonely man when most at the age of 42 already had a sweetheart or a wife. For the six months he had been going there, the same waitress served him, a lonely shy girl of 35 who had a secret crush on him but didn't know how to express it. Mom suggested something that would soon change their lives forever. For the first time a fortune cookie was placed next to his dessert of a small bowl of ice cream. Michael was curious and cracked open the cookie to read a short message that was printed especially for him ahead of time. Nancy the waitress stood just behind him as it was read. "Love is just around the corner." He walked outside and then around the block to see if it was there. There was nothing to be seen, so Michael went back inside to give a tip that was previously forgotten. Mom pointed to the kitchen and said "my daughter, your waitress would like to see you." It was just around the corner from where he sat as Nancy stood there with his fortune cookie in her hands. By this time the place had closed except for him and her just looking at each other for the first time. Mom waited outside as she heard the sounds of a silent kiss from two lonely souls. On loves path we take a ride every Sunday to fill our hunger and something more. Just around the corner but not necessarily outside and around the block. For Michael and Nancy it was indoors from a table to a kitchen. The shy and the lonely share love sometimes at a table where dessert sits along with a fortune cookie....

Ahead Of Time...

It's not just a screen name but a real live person. The buddy list and addresses may vanish but the person still exists. For those who were once close let them always remain. You never know when paths may cross again in real life. They filled up a tank of gas in a station not too far away from each other. An introduction happened once again with familiar faces smiling at each other. So a memory is kept alive and never lost between those who type and those who drive. A vacancy sign was read just up the road, a place to stop for those who made a reservation ahead of time....

The Playground...

A writer read his own last short story from his third book "On loves Path." It was so real to him that he decided to take this piece of fiction and live it out as best he could. Michael took the book with him to a place which was a playground from another time in his childhood. Her name and face were still embedded in his heart from where two young kids sat on a see saw a long time ago. A first crush or love that faded like old black and white photos from a grammar school graduation year book. It was a Sunday afternoon when school was closed as the writer sat on a see saw and thought about her. On a bench in that same playground a lady about the same age as him was reading the last story of a book called "On loves Path." His face and name were not too far away sitting on a see saw where she once sat also. They called each others name from a short distance where this particular Sunday had them together once again. Two adults with a childhood memory sat on both ends of a see saw and rode up and down in a playground from the final story of a writer's book....

Not A Day Goes By...

Not a day goes by without me thinking of you. We never met in person, yet for now a dream will do when I awake with a smile. Somehow a morning cup of coffee or a cold glass of orange juice has our fingerprints on it. Not a day goes by when I kiss you hello and wait to kiss you again upon my return. A red rose that sat on my kitchen table now sits in a vase that you prepared ahead of time. For others we never met before, but for me it is as real as can be. I love you so much and not a day goes by....

An Old Spiral Notebook...

It started and ended with an old spiral notebook written and found. Hand written short stories and poems that filled it from cover to cover in faded but readable blue ink. A hobby to pass the time for a homeless man we shall call Mickey. Just a block away it was lost on a busy midtown street where he used to buy coffee before going back to the shelter of his darkened alleyway. He retraced his steps but the old spiral notebook was nowhere to be found. Mickey noticed a few weeks later a well dressed woman about his own age walking out of the same coffee shop he went to. She was holding an old spiral notebook and reading it as she paused to read the last page. "Hey, that's my notebook," he screamed with joy in a hoarse voice. "And you are?" she asked. His signature was the same as the name he replied. Sharon introduced herself and complimented the homeless Mickey on his writings. He adjusted the worn blue tie on his wrinkled white shirt and said "thank you." She handed him a hundred dollar bill and said "get yourself cleaned up, buy some clothes, and then meet me here." Mickey took her business card to find out she was the president of a major publishing company. A haircut and beard trim followed along with a hot shower and new clothes. A new man entered her office and sat across the desk from which she was about to speak. "We cleaned up some misspelled words and such, but all and all I believe your writings can sell a book for us and of course you will profit also." Six months later the book flew off the shelves and Mickey returned her phone call of the good news. He adjusted his brand new blue tie on his new clean white shirt as he accepted a proposed date from her. Sharon said yes when he handed her a ring the following year and even autographed a book for her with a title that read "an old spiral notebook"....

Click Return and Then Save...

Screams of help had me jump out of my car a block before arriving home. Three thugs were attacking an elderly woman as each was grabbing for her pocketbook that was strapped around her shoulder. My combat training from a long forgotten war in Vietnam kicked into my brain and I quickly subdued and two of the three attackers as the third fled from the scene. 911 was called by a witness and the police took into custody two of the three muggers. Eventually the third was caught as he was ratted out by the other two. Evelyn and I got to know each other over the next couple weeks as a lonely pair of 60 year olds talked about our past. She was a nurse back in those days who saved many soldiers, one of them being me. Our focus of memories became clear as I remembered her and she remembered me. How strange we met again so many years later as I saved her life after she saved mine. My old soldiers uniform still fit as so did her nurses uniform. They were the outfits of a bride and a groom in a special wedding ceremony performed this year. Maybe in God's plan there is a button or two which clicks on "Return and then save." On loves path a healed soldier and a life saving nurse meet once again. Maybe we all wear uniforms from a different time, yet never change them when the time is right. Case in point written by an author called God who clicks on "Return and then save"....

A Gap in the Bridge...

The clock in my car read 2 AM and traffic across the bridge was nearly non-existent. A right blinker flashed in front of me when its driver changed from the middle to the right lane. Then the double warning lights flashed as it stopped and the driver got out on the passenger side door. I stopped behind it thinking it must be some car trouble and maybe I could help. A young lady stepped over the railing to the walkway and lifted her foot to climb onto the edge of the bridge. This was not car trouble, but a suicide about to happen. I took a deep breath and just started to speak with whatever words would help. "You don't know me, what the hell are you doing here?" she screamed in a drunken stupor. "You took my spot, I was going to jump from here," I replied. The young lady laughed out loud and said "should I move a few feet to give you room?" I sat beside her on the edge of the bridge and looked down at the cold water below. "Didn't you see the sign no jumping off the bridge without a swim suit?" She laughed once again and replied "you know something mister; I'm beginning to like you." The other traffic just kept on moving along as we talked for another hour or two about why we should go home. "We can hold hands now and jump, or maybe hold hands in the morning over breakfast," I said. She picked the latter idea and we drove home back to her place in my car of course with her sleeping in the back seat. Breakfast was followed by lunch and dinner and many weeks and months of dating. A life was saved and that is all that matters to me. There was a return trip over a bridge which we needed to cross in order to get to our wedding. A bridge to gap that brought us together in the first place. On loves path maybe a blinker and flashing red lights lead us to give a helping hand. A couple of laughs restore the need to survive and live once again. Case in point, a gap in the bridge....

Mary Jo Beth...

Mary Jo Beth, country girl born and raised in the mountains of Tennessee. A former tomboy who used to climb trees and catch fish in blue overalls with red pigtails flopping in the breeze, now at twenty-one she sits and waits for a plane to take her to a city she had never been to before. Her new attire was a dress that mom bought for her before she left the nest she grew up in. Outside the window and just below was the airport as the plane made its final approach. She brushed her now straight red hair and applied a little makeup before leaving the exit ramp. I picked up my banjo as the rest of my suitcases waited on the revolving ramp. A cab drove me to the hotel that I was to live at for the next couple of weeks. The big city welcomed me with my first audition at a country and western bar located in downtown Manhattan. My singing voice and banjo playing won over the crowd and after a few months I became very popular in downtown Manhattan. An agent from a major record company sat in the crowd one night and approached me as I was packing up to go home. My name is Jim Bob and I signed this young talent to a five year deal as her first album went gold. We never talked of personal stuff, it was always strictly business. Maybe it was her light green eyes and red hair that made me ask a few questions. Amazingly we found out that we both grew up and were raised in the mountains of Tennessee. I used to fish and climb trees with her and we even had back then our first kiss. The engagement ring was given and accepted some months later by Mary Jo Beth. Jim Bob smiled from the wedding hall as his wife picked up her banjo and played their favorite song. On love's path we have those who leave and return to a place they have never been before. Case in point where distance and time have special results for Mary Jo Beth....

The Request...

A screen name and an email sometimes becomes a dream. I wonder about the real live person who types on their keyboard. Words in person are so close, so far away. I often share a cup of coffee with you in the morning and click glasses at night in a toast of our meeting. To look in your eyes and speak without saying a word is all I ask....

Country Roads...

There I was, pulling into a gas station about one mile away from the hotel where I would be staying. A John Denver song played on the radio called "Country Roads." It was quite an amazing coincidence that he was singing about West Virginia, the place I was in. Across from me another car sat at another pump and I had to stare at her for a moment before she became a familiar face. It was pretty much the same as a picture posted by her on a web site where people would write to each other. She turned her head and looked at me with the same recognition of seeing my face before. "I can't believe it, is that you Michael?" She asked as her window rolled down. "Dianna?" I said at the same time. We pulled out of the gas station and parked by the side of the road where we could talk. It turned out that she was a buddy who read my short stories online and replied with the most sincere and wonderful compliments. My 2 week vacation became an unexpected pleasure of having met her in person. We spent as much time as possible together during my visit until I had to drive back to New York. She sat next to me in my car before we had to say goodbye. I was hoping this first kiss wasn't our last. With five minutes she turned the radio on in my car. It was no longer a coincidence when a John Denver song played once again a song called "Country Roads." On loves path we have a time and a place where both are supposed to be. A special song plays twice which has them both know that they will be together again....

As A Child At Heart Often Does...

It was third grade and I chased her around the playground as we laughed and held hands before going back to class. There was a daily kiss on the cheek and secret love notes passed under desks just before the bell rang to let us out of school. So those innocent childhood memories led me back to the school where it all started. Now a young adult at 21, I still felt like that little boy flirting with that dream once again. This particular Saturday afternoon someone else was thinking and dreaming of the same thing. She was lot taller now but there was that same twinkle in those light blue eyes that belonged to her some 18 years ago. I chased her around the playground and when she stood still for a moment to catch her breath, we kissed on the lips. It was under other desks that we passed love notes and other places we still held hands. The outdoor wedding took place in a public park just across from the school we used to attend. About five minutes after we said our vows, the guests followed us to watch the groom chase the bride around a playground just across the street. They applauded when we kissed as kids and adults at the same time. I held her hand as a child at heart often does. On loves path we take a memory and go visit it once again. Sometimes the other does the same....

Arizona Doll...

I just needed a full tank of gas and an oil change. A task that would take about 45 minutes at the station I pulled into. It was on a main highway that led through Arizona where the stop was made before I reached the final destination a state away. A small souvenir shop sat across the street, and so to kill some time I checked out what may be interesting to bring back home. A foot tall Indian doll caught my attention with her original dress included. The old man with gray hair and a red bandana around his forehead approached the cash register and smiled at me with a few tears in his eyes. "What you hold is a hand made carving of my granddaughter who left me about five or six years ago. Her real hair that I saved was used in the making of this Arizona doll." "Maybe you should keep it and not sell this memory of her," I said. "Take it my young friend and pay nothing, for maybe this is what is supposed to be." I drove to the final state where my vacation was to take place with the Arizona doll beside me in the front seat. There was a hitchhiker standing in the road just before the state she was trying to get to. She just pointed to where her destination was as I stopped abruptly when the doll was the exact likeness of the old mans missing granddaughter. My car did a U turn and I explained why we needed to go back from where it came. She put her head on my shoulder and slept the rest of the way there. The old man watched the both of us get out of my car and smiled at something that maybe he knew ahead of time. Grandpa and granddaughter hugged and kissed for five years that were lost. Maybe it was an old Indian custom, maybe something else. I'll never know for sure, but her hand in marriage was offered to me by the grandfather. I accepted and we became man and wife soon afterwards. Grandpa still keeps the figure in his souvenir shop though it is not for sale anymore. I sleep now with the real Arizona doll....

Emily's Rose...

Two stick figures were drawn but you could tell which was the boy and which was the girl. He held his outstretched hand to her with a rose as his name and her name were printed above their heads. The torn out page from his notebook was handed to the girl sitting in front of him. She turned around with a smile and that was a sign that she accepted his gift. It was Emily's rose. Many years later maybe by fate, she ended up sitting in front of him in High School. It was Valentines Day and he wrote a special love poem to her inside the card. On the cover was a beautiful red rose. She turned around with a smile and that was a sign that she accepted his gift. It was Emily's rose. Some years later maybe by fate she ended up sitting in front of him in college. There was no special occasion except for the fact of him being deeply in love with her. Nobody noticed when she turned around and leaned over to give him a special kiss. It was Emily's rose. Not too far from then he was at her house on a regular but special date. One hand was behind his back and the other held an engagement ring. She said yes and then took a red flower that the other hand was holding. It was Emily's rose. There were many years that followed for the bride and groom until old age caught up to the happy couple. She passed away from natural causes and I laid down a special flower on her coffin. It wasn't in mourning, but a celebration of the life we had together. It was Emily's rose. On loves path we show our affection to those who may sit in front of us by fate or choice. It comes in the form of stick figures with an outstretched hand, then a photo on the cover of a card. Then the actual flower that reminds me of love given and received. In loving memory of Emily's rose....

Party Doll...

Madeline put on her makeup, fluffed her hair and pranced out the door for another night out. Whether it be a bowling alley, a wedding, or just plain bar hopping, she was a party girl. Drinks and jokes and laughter mixed in with some flirting usually had her at the center of attention. It seemed she could leave with anybody she wanted to, but always left alone. Maybe she tried too hard and that scared some away. Harold usually had to be dragged out by his friends and always sat in a corner somewhere unnoticed. He was shy but usually went along for the ride. At a dance club they met when she tripped and fell just outside the ladies room. He was coming out of the men's room a few feet away and helped her back to her feet. Harold just smiled with his shy eyes and walked back up the stairs to the main floor. Madeline was surprised to see a guy that didn't hit on her and try to get fresh. A change of pace that attracted her to him. She bought a drink for Harold and the two sat there and talked until the place was about to close. For the first time, both left together not alone. An unlikely couple, except for those who believe opposites attract. They somehow met in the middle after some months together as she wouldn't put on as much makeup as she once did, nor fluff her hair. He became more outgoing and told a few jokes once in a while as love blossomed and eventually became a marriage. My name is Harold and I wrote this about my party doll....

A Written Kiss...

The tool is a keyboard which types letters, words, and paragraphs. It reaches those with the same power as the spoken word. Imagery is brought to life and feelings are felt not just from the eyes, but the heart as well. We are connected with a bond as if we have known each other all our lives. Therefore I leave for now with a written kiss....

The Postman Delivers...

It was a time before computers and chats and emails. The year was 1958 when we licked a postage stamp and placed it in the right hand corner of an envelope. The postman delivers and we read a response to that which was sent. For Janet and Robert it was letters exchanged that summer while she was away at a summer camp a state away. High school sweethearts staying in touch for July and August while temporarily being separated. Her replies to his mail became less frequent as a secret summer love occupied her time. Then it stopped altogether. He never saw her during their senior year and she avoided his phone calls as it soon became obvious that she met somebody else. Robert never stopped thinking about her even after graduating college. He took a postal exam and passed as the new mail carrier for his district. Janet's house was on his daily route and he took a chance on her still living there. His blue uniform was cleaned and pressed for what he hoped would be a special time in his life. It was a Sunday morning when mail is not delivered as Janet answered the front door. He stood before her with a dozen roses and said nothing except for the tears which ran down his cheeks. Janet did the same and hugged a first love she hoped would eventually return. On loves path we lick a few stamps until our tongue goes dry. Then we show up in a place needed to be once again. Nothing else needs to be said, just felt from where it all began....

The Last Entry...

It sat in the bottom of a drawer in the back corner under some socks. An item forgotten that was placed there about ten years ago. I blew off the dust and opened an old address book from those bar hopping days and nights. It was about half full with names and numbers with addresses in now faded blue ink. Next to each name was a check mark, an X, or a question mark to describe how the date went. The last entry caught my attention as no notation was made except for "this number has been temporarily disconnected." She was not a one night stand and her name brought back familiar feelings of falling in love. Her drawer open as she searched for a clean pair of underwear. In the back corner was an old address book her hand touched as she picked it up and blew off the dust that accumulated over the last ten years. The last entry was what caught her attention. It was just his name with a faded number that could no longer be read. A feeling of a once forgotten love that may have been had crossed her mind. The doorbell rang as she clutched it in her hand and opened the front door. "Hello, we met briefly about ten years ago and I still love you," he said with a tear running down his cheek. She smiled and said "yes, I remember you too and never stopped loving you." They showed each a last entry from each others address book and spoke of how it was that now it had become the first. A reservation was made for a wedding hall where they signed the last entry. On loves path the ten years waited for a couple that was supposed to be. It can be found sometimes in the back of a drawer where we need to look for a morning change of socks or underwear. Blow off the dust and look at the last entry....

Aisle Five, Breakfast Cereals...

Aisle five, "breakfast cereals." That was my first stop in the supermarket to stock up on frosted flakes. We leaned down together as our hand grabbed the same box without us noticing that the other was there. "You can take it, I'll have the one next to it," I said to her. She smiled and we both turned around once more to look at each other before waving a temporary good bye. My next shopping spree came about the same time again when things were running low. I was hoping she would be there again even though the odds were against it. Her voice from behind me said "you take that box; I'll take the one next to it." We spent the next hour walking down various aisles together talking and picking up items we really didn't need. It was a Friday afternoon and we made a date to meet that night. She put the single red rose I had bought in a vase on the kitchen table before we left her house. It was the best date I ever had and she said the same thing. An invitation to come in her house after our date was accepted. We awoke that Saturday morning together as she asked me if I felt like some breakfast. Both our hands held a box of frosted flakes and shook it as we shared the same bowl along with a few more kisses. On loves path we shop and sometimes meet someone without looking. The odds are against a second time on the same day, but yet love is not an odds maker. It does what is supposed to be done, sometimes in aisle five, "breakfast cereals"....

Julia...

She stood in my display window where I dressed her often throughout the seasons. A mannequin who sold clothes and jewelry and such with special lighting and props that I have personally set up. She may have been just of wood with different wigs, but to me this display was something more. We have here a display manager who is lonely with no social life and no girlfriends. He takes comfort in talking to a dummy who he believes in his mind to be a real live person. Michael prepared the window in the department store he worked on it for a wedding gown to be displayed in June, just one week away. He bought an ankle chain with his name and hers, Julia, and carefully attached it to her left foot. The gown was sold out by mid July as a big promotion along with a huge raise was presented to him. On the way to work the following morning, he helped a young lady who was trying to change her flat tire. "You look like someone who I have known before," he said. "My name is Julia, and you look very familiar also." she replied. He noticed just below her left pants leg was something there that needed to be looked at. A mannequin that was supposed to be there when he got to work was no longer in the display window. On loves path we have a lonely worker with an imaginary girlfriend. Her name and the chain around her left ankle confirmed something. Love between those who are real and those imagined sometimes meet in a place in between. Just ask the bride and groom in a display window next time you pass by....

Just In Case...

Our son turned 26 years old and he decided to move out. For mom it was very emotional as mother and son always have that special connection. We kissed him goodbye but he was only just 20 minutes away in his new apartment. The bedroom he used to sleep in was now a den and a work place for the wife. I cried to myself at night as memories of growing up and playing together filled my mind. A teddy bear I used to tuck in with him, a catch of football in the back yard. Some twenty years later an ad was answered to fill a vacant room for rent. Two old people invited the man in as he held a football and a teddy bear. We cried with open arms and said 'welcome home son." I threw the football again in the backyard and he caught my pass. He asked me to bring a teddy bear to hug once again as I tucked him in. On loves path we have those who leave the nest and sometimes eventually return. Keep your football and a teddy bear just in case....

The Fireplace...

The fireplace burned out a long time ago but was still there. It existed in a cabin where a week of memories was too strong to ignore. The winter of 1970 was revisited in 1990 at the vacation resort where it all began. I rented the exact same cabin and picked up the standard bible left on a nightstand beside the bed. Something fell out of it that I forgot to pack 20 years earlier. It was a picture of the girl who loved me that entire week where the fireplace burned. My tears soaked a pillow and dreams had me wish of her returning. Maybe the clerk at the front desk made a mistake, maybe not. She put the key in a cabin door that was stayed at where a memory had her go back to. I let her in as she held a photo she put in a bible that she remembered to pack. The fireplace suddenly lit by itself and we neither questioned nor ignored it. Another week together that would last for the rest of all winters to come. 1991 was a year where a honeymoon took place just a winter away. We bought a house and made sure to always light the fireplace. On loves path we have our favorite seasons and our favorite memories. When two check into a memory then all is never forgotten. Keep a match or lighter ready, for you never know when the cold becomes warm once again in the fireplace....

Halloween revisited...

It was a favorite time growing up with a special occasion at the end of October. Dressing up in a different costume each year on Halloween and going door to door for trick or treat. It was those years of being together with someone who made it all worth while. She was a neighbor named Doris who walked with me down the street as we held hands. We would fill our bags with treats but I would put most of mine into hers when she wasn't looking. A few kisses on the cheek were exchanged until we finally grew up and moved away to another location. Next week is Halloween as I now long to go back to the street where it all happened. At 30 years old, I picked out a costume that would fit an adult and drove about an hour to where I once lived. My Prince Charming outfit fit perfectly and felt comfortable as some of the adults there also dressed up to go trick or treating. A lady in a Cinderella costume came back to a street she used to live on many years ago. Doris said "remember me?" I replied "how can I ever forget you?" We held hands as I snuck my treats into her bag when she wasn't looking. On loves path we have a children's favorite holiday that needed to be revisited once again. A diamond engagement ring was a gift accepted not from knocking on doors, but from an occasion where those who need to meet again....

China Doll...

Just about a mile away from the new neighborhood I moved into was a Chinese restaurant. Since it was the closest, why not give it a try? The waitress was about the same age as me, give or take a year of me being 25. It was her friendly smile that I noticed first and then her expressive light green eyes. In a soft voice she said "I'll be back to take your order in a few minutes as you look at our menu." "I'll have the pork fried rice with a bowl of wonton soup and an egg roll," I said as she came back to take my order. The food was fantastic and I became a regular customer every Friday night. There was no more need for a menu as she knew what I liked and the order was always placed ahead of time just before my nine pm arrival. An elderly lady approached my table and said "I am the owner of this restaurant your waitress happens to be my daughter. She is and has been attracted to you for some time now, but is too shy to say so. Will you please ask her out for a date?" "I most certainly will, thank you for telling me," I replied. Next Saturday we had a date at an American restaurant where for the first time she had a cheeseburger and fries. Her smile told me that she enjoyed herself that evening and her light green eyes sparkled like never before. After some months of dating her mom approached me before I left her restaurant. "My daughter has fallen in love with you and all I ask is that you do the right thing." "I promise that will be done," was my reply. A special large fortune cookie was baked by her mom at my request. The girl who I fell in love with sat across from me on her day off that her mom had arranged. The fortune cookie was cracked open and my engagement ring fell out. Her light green eyes swelled with tears of joy and she said the word "yes" about ten times as mom came out of the kitchen to congratulate us. The wedding was about half Chinese and half American and so was the food. I ate my pork fried rice with an egg roll and wonton soup as my bride enjoyed her cheeseburger and fries. On top of the wedding cake our small statues sat with a smile. Next to me was my China doll. On loves path we have a new neighborhood with a new restaurant. A customer and a waitress from different cultures. Yet similar eyes and smiles shine where love binds us together. Thanks mom for your China doll….

More Or Less...

We love from a distant place maybe in a dream or our thoughts. I call your name as you call mine and then the phone rings at the same time a knock on our front doors. To speak in person and gaze in each others eyes. Just a hug and a kiss is all I ask, nothing more and nothing less....

The Same Footprints...

Another New Years coming up with the company of a bottle and a remote control for the T V, those were the thoughts of a lonely young man who should have somebody by now. His boots left footprints on the way to the usual liquor store in another snow filled sidewalk just like the year before. He made it there just about five minutes before it was to be closed. Less than twenty feet away from the store, he turned around to see her pounding on the front door. The young man turned around and walked towards the girl who was too late to buy what she needed. He pulled his bottle out of the shopping bag and said "if you have no other plans tonight, we can share this together?" "That's the same exact bottle I was going to buy," she replied. It turned out she had no plans as she walked back home with him to his place, a thought that she had also about another New Years coming up with a bottle and a remote control soon left her mind. No footprints left the house during the few days of the snowstorm as this new couple spent the next few months together. In June she became his bride and the man at the liquor store down the block was invited for special reasons of their own. It was an outdoor wedding on a beach where two people shared the same footprints. On loves path we find a store open for one but closes for another. Yet one has what the other was going to buy and much more....

Eyes Of The Heart...

The beauty and wonders which surrounds us can only be appreciated through the eyes of the heart. When it listens to a waterfall, it can be seen also. And so I dream of you without having to listen, to see, for all is needed to feel. The eyes of the heart shall never close....

Paper Airplanes...

After the love poem was written, I folded the notebook paper into the popular airplane shape and flung it in her direction. It guided itself onto the desk in front of her maybe some ten feet away. Such is the way of one shy grade school boy sharing his love. She turned around as I waved and smiled so now it was known where it came from. The same paper airplane hit me later in back of the head upon leaving class at the end of day. A poem of her own filled up the remaining space along with a red crayon drawing of red lips which to me meant a kiss. Our graduation photo album had us standing next to each other holding hands. She giggled through high school and college as the paper airplanes continued to fly her way. I was shipped off to the Vietnam War and became a pilot in the airborne division. Missing in action was a telegram that was sent and for many nights she cried. One year after the war was over I awoke in a hospital back in the states. No records were found of how or why I ended up where I did, but maybe only God or his angels had a plan. She sat at her kitchen table with the window open one summer as something flew in and landed on the table in front her. She read an original love poem from a blank piece of notebook paper that said what was needed for her to hear. We hugged and kissed after I knocked on her door. The wedding was different from others as instead of glasses clicking for the bride and groom to kiss, there were paper airplanes thrown about. On loves path maybe all it takes is a love poem and a red crayon to reply with a kiss....

Door Of The Heart...

Behind you I stand as sometimes eyes do not see in front of us. Remember the tap on your shoulder when nobody was there. Capture my image in a dream and forget it not when five minutes after awakening it fades. Words that are typed or written shall eventually be spoken when the door of the heart is opened....

Fawn...

It wasn't that I saved a life, but prevented one from being taken away. On the road to a camping trip which wound through some curves, a small baby deer froze as it stood in front of my headlights. I slammed the brakes and swerved into the other lane as my car came to a stop. In my rear view mirror the baby deer was shaking, then stared back at me with what looked like a smile. She trotted off into the woods as I thanked God neither one of us was injured or killed. Luckily no cars were coming in my direction as I pulled back into the right lane. From the parking area at the resort, I had to walk to the campgrounds about five minutes away. My tent was set up and just outside of it the campfire burned. I got lost while walking too deep into the woods not realizing my exploring had taken me too far from camp. A baby deer peeked from behind a tree as she caught my attention. She walked slowly and kept turning her head around to make sure I was following her, which I did. There was a small glow of amber red ashes about fifty feet away which was left of the campfire from a few hours before. Her head bobbed up and down as if she knew I returned to where I would be safe once again. I called to her with a name "forest fawn" which my mind made up when we first met. She approached me as I took off the chain from around my neck and put it on hers. One year later the incident was forgotten by my brain, but not my heart. A young lady came up to me at a dance club and said "can we have this slow dance together?" I replied, "Yes, of course." A gold chain sat around her neck and she introduced herself as fawn". On loves path we avoid a possible tragedy and then find out a way to get back home. Maybe nature comes in many different forms of love that is needed to be continued....

If Only One Is Touched...

If only one is touched by a story or a poem then so be it. After all, that one will touch others. My books and writings have reached many but it is the quality and not the quantity where it counts the most. No royalty or sales are on my mind, just the few who have smiled and gone to bed with a happy thought. For those who reply, thank you, for those who have not, then maybe just one who you know will mention it. If only one is touched....

A Bird Called Bernie...

Dad bought me a parakeet for my eighth birthday, a baby with green and black feathers and a blue beak that would soon learn and repeat words which I taught him. It was a bird called Bernie, the name I had given him. My new friend had spoken several simple phrases over the next few months such as "hello, good morning, kiss me and hungry now." He eventually would sit on my finger when I placed my hand into his cage. After about a year, we let him come out and fly around the kitchen but Bernie would always return to his cage on his own. Four years later it was habit that he sat on my shoulder and pecked on my ear gently as I knew it was just a kiss. Bernie sometimes sat on the edge of a bowl at dinner time and picked up a noodle or two from my chicken soup. He was my best friend, my pet and I loved him dearly. Eight years went by and on my sixteenth birthday I woke up to feed him and give fresh water. He lay on his back on the bottom of the cage with his feet curled up and his eyes closed. Mom and dad had to hold me as I shook and cried for quite a long time. In the backyard he was buried with a cross I taped together with two toothpicks. My parents kept the cage in the kitchen at my request, for I knew somehow he would return. I packed my books for school one Monday morning and sat down for a quick breakfast. It was just a two word phrase that I heard very distinctly, but none that was taught. Bernie said "don't go." I told my parents that I felt sick and couldn't make it to school that morning. They called up and had me listed as absent for a sick day. The school bus turned over that morning on a rain slicked road where the driver was going too fast. Thirty eight students died that morning as the flames consumed the bus from a leaking gas tank. The cage in my kitchen had a few green and black feathers which were not previously there. On loves path we have a little boy and his pet parakeet. Not many phrases but a few that were learned were spoken. A new one was chirped which saved his life that morning which only he heard. Case in point between my love and his from a bird called Bernie....

Vivian's Return...

Her hair was growing back and she started to feel like her old self once again. The chemotherapy and her will to live won the battle of cancer. I know this because she sent me mail. Vivian and I were close friends some years back as we worked in the same investment firm in midtown Manhattan. My thoughts here in this story probably reflect the same memories as hers. She was a receptionist on a floor I delivered mail to. We hit it off from the beginning and I would often be a little late in delivering the mail due to our chats at her desk. I remember buying a T V guide for her on most Fridays so she could check what's on for the following week. After a while, security was beefed up in our building and cameras were installed all over the place. My chats with her became limited as we joked about "big brother" watching us. However we did have some time alone together after work when meeting for a few drinks at a local bar. Eventually we both got laid off and sort of lost contact with each other. Then I got the mail from her about how she loved my stories and thought I was a very good writer. She requested me to write a story about her and so here it is as you all read this. It will be published in my third book so here is sneak preview. We now fast forward to a summer resort some years later. It was in the state she lived in and who would have thought that we would end up there both on the exact same weekend. Vivian sat on a lounge chair in the outdoor pool. She was reading my third book "On Loves Path" when I approached her and said "that book looks like it needs an autograph by the author." She smiled and cried at the same time as I did the same. "Let me get a drink, I'll be right back." Vivian stood up and walked to the outdoor bar at the pool after placing a bookmark in the page that was to be continued. Out of curiosity I opened it to see where she had left off. It was a story that I promised to write for her, "Vivian's Return"....

5 Minutes...

If only I had 5 minutes with you, we can cover a lifetime. Words need not to be spoken, just thoughts and feelings. Are you too far away or was my pillow not next to yours anymore? Look outside your window and see someone who will knock or ring a bell. Remember a dream if only you had 5 minutes...?

Porch Dweller...

Joe and his wife were my next door neighbors on the main floor of a condo we all lived in. He was an elderly gentleman who enjoyed sitting on the front porch that we shared with him on the left and me on the right. Joe would sit there with his newspaper and his wife sip on a cup of coffee as they talked in between. He walked with a cane for, my guess was, a bum leg and maybe a bad back also. My wife would usually visit his on weekend mornings for coffee and chat. One day I was sitting on the porch on my side and watched him get up to go back into his house. It was only one step up to reach the door, but I noticed that with his cane he was struggling to go up and in. "Don't move Joe, I'll be right there to help you." He took my arm and managed to hoist himself up that step. Then he lost balance and started to fall to the side, but I caught him and finally got him into his house. That night I kept thinking to my self "I hope someone is there when he walks down the two steps to street level to get to his car." He shouldn't be alone and may need help. Maybe a week later before my wife went to work that morning, she told me that Joe fell down the steps the night before and cracked his head open. My heart sunk and as my stomach had a sick feeling. The front porch was a place Joe enjoyed as long as the weather was decent out of the twelve months of the year along with his wife. He passed away and I cried even though he and I never really said much to each other except a hello or how you doing? The following spring his wife sat at their table on the front porch. I looked at her from my open front door and heard her talking to the empty chair next to her which used to be his. Maybe I thought she was just talking to herself until I noticed a newspaper on the table in front of him. There was no wind or breeze that morning, yet I saw with my own eyes a page turn. Then they both continued their chat as I smiled and went back into my house....

A Song, A Dance, And A Blanket...

The beach was still there of course even though the crowd was now different. It wasn't too far to drive where I used to live and so I spread out the blanket, turned on an oldies station, then dozed off to memories of what used to be. In my dream the old crowd was there and a favorite song came on that my girl and I used to dance to. It was a slow one and after that we held hands on the blanket and kissed as the sun went down. I knew this was a dream and wondered why it was taking so long for me to wake up. There was a tap on my shoulder from a woman who said "It's getting late dear and you were sleeping long enough. Let's go home now." She was an older version of my first love I had lost a long time ago. Her name was the same and I didn't question what had just happened to me on that beach we used to go to. On one hand was my high school ring; on the other was a wedding band. Before we left a song played and we did another slow dance. The sun set again on a blanket where we still held hands. On loves path we sometimes mix up or combine the past and present. The result may be in the future on a beach we used to go to. Don't think too hard about this story; just bring a song, a dance, and a blanket....

Central Park Picnic...

The year was 1968 and it was a fine early summer day on a Sunday afternoon. The green grass and some colorful flowers spread cheer over this place known as Central Park. I spread the picnic blanket just underneath a tree that provided enough shade from the hot afternoon sun. Another did the same about a hundred feet away under her own shaded tree. About the same time we each popped open our beverage; mine a can of beer, hers the cork from a bottle of wine. We looked at each other from that distance every now and then even though we couldn't make out what the other actually looked like. At one point she raised her glass of wine and I raised my can of beer to acknowledge each other in a toast from the distance. The next couple of Sundays our blankets seemed to get closer and closer until we could actually see each others face and smile. Finally we met in person as two shy people often do until one of them makes a first move. It was now late August and we both sat on the same blanket under the same tree. Several kisses could be heard by the birds chirping around us. The year was 1970 and the parks department approved an outdoor wedding on their grounds. We stood under a shaded tree that Month of June and said our wedding vows. Cans and bottles were popped open as toasts were made by guests and onlookers alike. It may have been an unusual title for our wedding album, but it was appropriate enough for us. "Central Park Picnic." On loves path we have sometimes a distance of two blankets in a park. Each Sunday they get closer and closer until the occupants recognize each other. Green grass and colorful flowers are just a backdrop to any place we eventually meet. It is the two who decide what to do with each other that paints the whole picture....

It Was Just A Goodnight...

It was just a goodnight spoken to someone far away in another city or state. Not over the phone, but in a whisper next to his pillow before going to sleep. He never met her before in person, she was just somebody he knew who responded to his short stories and poems. Her picture was there and it often crossed his mind as he would see her in his heart. They both felt the same way yet knew not of this. On the same night a dream was shared where they met in a shopping mall in an aisle where leather gloves were sold. The dream was forgotten until one cold November day she was on the way to visit some relatives who she hadn't seen in quite a while. There stood a new mall about a block away from her destination and she decided that it was time for a new pair of gloves. A familiar dream surfaced and she turned around to see him standing behind her. He was on the way to visit some relatives who he hadn't seen in quite a while. A new mall caught his eye and he thought to himself about needing a new pair of leather gloves. A familiar dream surfaced as she stood in front of him. They agreed to get together after the plans of meeting their relatives that Thanksgiving holiday. The Xmas tree was lit and he opened a small black box with a ring that she accepted. There was a whisper for real this time next to his pillow before going to sleep. It said "I love you." On loves path we take a turn and get off where some new gloves are needed. A dream before which was forgotten until it had to happen for those wanting to remember. It was just a goodnight....

Return Receipt Requested...

It had been so long since she last communicated with him. His screen name was forgotten years ago but Michael remained in her memory of dreams. Their plans to meet some time ago were shattered by distance and circumstances which often are the obstacles we find on the computer. He thought of her often also as the same dreams occurred about her. His lost screen name of the girl he once loved was still a first name he remembered also. Wendy passed by a book store and went in as she browsed the new selection of just released books. His old photo was on the back cover as his third book was there. The years before when she knew him, was a time when neither knew he would become a famous author and writer. Wendy purchased his third book "On Loves Path" and ordered his first two also. Her name was written in one short story from each of his books and she knew then how he missed and felt about her. Certified mail with return receipt requested was sent to his address. Michael signed for it and read the 3 page letter enclosed. Tears came to his eyes but were wiped dry enough to write down the phone number that was at the end of the letter. It was at least a two hour conversation they had as plans were made to meet once again. She rang his doorbell as he helped her bring in the two suitcases of luggage which they would unpack and put away together. A second pillow was bought the following day where her head rested next to his. On loves path we lose a screen name over the years but remember their real first name. Dreams of each other kept both alive until a book store finally had them meet again. Love lost and found in a short story called "return receipt requested"....

For What Else...

Your lips are just a kiss away. Your arms are just a hug away. So how far do we need to become closer? Maybe a dream that binds the miles between two pillows, maybe something more. I call your name in sleeping and waking moments for what else is there for me to do?

Hospitals And Flowers...

I awoke in the recovery room after surgery from a critical car accident. My blurry eyes came into focus on a small table next to my bed which was in arms reach. A card was taped to a tall vase that contained a few red roses. The nurse came in and asked if he would like her to read him the card. I nodded yes as she opened it. "I was in surgery helping the doctor as best I could and said a prayer for your life. Maybe my feelings had something to do with it." It was signed by someone that had a nametag I didn't notice at the time. Two months later I had to go back to the hospital, not for an injury but to thank the nurse who gave me those flowers and a card which maybe had just saved my life. Her shift was over and my angel now in street clothes still had her name tag on in my mind as her face was the same as before. I handed a vase with some flowers and a card attached which basically was a thank you for caring. We kissed when it was a time meant to be at a wedding where most of the guests were from a hospital staff that knew we would end up together. Her nametag was pinned to an album that we now look back on where it all began. On loves path a man goes into a hospital with his life on the line. A vase of flowers with a card and a prayer makes a difference. Love returns to where it was first sought, and then found once again....

At Any Time...

You are such a romantic; this story had me with a lump in my throat. You made me think and wonder and hope. Such was the one of the many positive comments which made me continue to write. It was heartfelt comments which were the whole purpose for me to do what I do. We need not meet in person to know each other, for in our mails we have touched in a more important way. If from that we have dreams of each other, then so be it. Maybe one day we will answer each others door for real. It remains unlocked on my end where one may enter at any time....

To Pass The Time...

It was one of the most boring places to be, but it had to get done. Washers and dryers would spin as customers dropped in their quarters as they sat and waited, and waited. I folded some items on the table and then packed everything into one large laundry bag. A lady started cursing just before I left so I stopped and looked at her and she looked at me at the same time. She just smiled and said "I'm short 2 quarters to finish my load." I had a few left and gave them to her and said "this should cover it". There was something about her I found very attractive but didn't know what or why. For some reason I was hoping she would be there the next time I was. A few weeks later I sat down with a book to read in order to pass the boring time at the laundromat. She was there again which defied the odds against it on the exact same day and time. The afternoon wasn't boring anymore as we sat together talked long after the machines had stopped spinning. Our plans were to meet again on specific days and times to keep each other company. The regular customers noticed us together after a few months of us sitting together and being somewhat affectionate. The round of applause drowned out the sound of the spinning machines as she said "yes" when I asked her to marry me. We own our own home together now with a washer and dryer included. The wife and I don't save quarters anymore but we still sit together to pass the time....

Melinda Of Maple Street...

There was block party I can remember in the summer of 1971. Tables of food and drink lined the street and neighbors got together who never really knew each other before. For me it was a girl named Melinda of Maple Street, the block that I lived on back then. Two kids who were 21 and 20 that would soon be first time lovers and friends. It took two years to get to know her really well as Melinda was a person who never cared for change or new things. She liked the same clothes and hair styles and we had that in common. I flew from the nest of my parent's house and found my own apartment some years later, but this girl remained in my thoughts and never left my heart. Twenty years have gone by and it just so happened that I had to travel through the old neighborhood where I once grew up. The houses looked the same and the cars were much newer now except for a 1971 Buick that was parked at the end of the street. She noticed my 1971 Ford park behind her as Melinda looked out her kitchen window. We stared at each other if only for a second or two as she came outside. The appointment I had was never kept, for something more important was needed to be done. She and I looked pretty much the same as we did before and kissed with a passion that was missed over the last twenty years. I ended up moving in with her on a street where it all began. I can remember a block party in the summer of 1992 where new and old neighbors gathered at an outdoor wedding. That was where I married my Melinda of Maple Street....

A Smooch Plus Hug...

The sign off was not a name, but a smooch plus hug, an affectionate way to be more personal. It carried over to many nights in dreams for both of them where mail had more meaning than just letters and sentences. You can hear and feel it in the distance when they met for the first time. A honeymoon follows where all is quiet except for a smooch plus hug....

Snowflakes, Slow Dances And Susan...

I don't usually set up something ahead of time unless there is a reason. In this case my intuition proved to be right as we shall see the following events unfold...Snowflakes started to fall just in time this particular Xmas Eve as I watched through the window pane from my kitchen. They glistened just below the street lights and became bigger and more intense. My gaze was interrupted by the ring of a doorbell which did not expect any company that night. She unwrapped the scarf from around her mouth as a vapor cloud whispered from her breath, "Hello...my name is Susan." The wind picked up and the snow became heavy as I asked her to come in. All she needed were some directions to a hotel she was to stay in for her visit to N. Y. The lost girl sat down after she took off her coat and I told her that I would get the directions from my computer and print them out for her. The snowflakes turned into a blizzard and I suggested she stay here for a while until it got better or stopped. Neither had occurred. Susan accepted a hot bowl of soup which we both had as our conversations had us lose track of time. We both agreed that it was not safe to continue driving and I would let her sleep over in my spare bedroom. Xmas songs played on my stereo and each time a slow one was on, we would dance to them. It felt like in those few hours that we had known each other all our lives. She looked at my Xmas tree and saw just one present beneath it. "So who is the gift for, and why are they not here?" she asked. "They arrived a few hours ago and are still here," I replied. Susan was a little puzzled as she watched me get up and pick up the present of my intuition from a month before. "I didn't know at the time who this was for, but it has become very clear to me tonight." I took a pen and wrote her name on the attached card as my hands gave it to her with a loving smile. It was an artificial red rose preserved in a Plexiglas case forever. Her tears were overwhelming, more so than any snowstorm could produce. Susan never made it to the hotel the next day, for she chose to stay with me instead. On loves path sometimes we have a hunch to buy something for a future event. Then directions that are needed to get somewhere become perfectly clear....

Counter Clockwise...

It didn't feel natural skating around the rink in a counter clockwise fashion. I felt sort of unbalanced and dizzy at times. However this was my first trip to the famous ice skating rink in Rockefeller Plaza and I wasn't going to let that get in my way of having a good time. After a few laps and a few falls, it became easier to adjust and I did alright the next hour or two. A new tourist entered the rink and slowly began skating as others passed her by. I stayed behind her and felt that she looked like she was about to fall at any time. Sure enough she did so and I helped her up at least three times during the next five laps. "I just can't seem to get used to this counter clockwise direction we are going. I feel dizzy sometimes and unbalanced" she said to me. We skated together for the next 45 minutes holding hands after we made our introductions of our names and where we were from. Our feet were finally tired enough that we had to take a break and sit down. Together we sat at an indoor bar and warmed up just inside where you can still view the rink from the bars window. Our sore feet wiggled below the bar stools with our shoes resting on the floor below. The rink finally closed but the bar and other shops were still open. My new friend and I ate there and were the last two left when the bartender announced his last call. It was on him as he smiled. We never exchanged phone numbers that night, it was just a chance meeting where we both had a good time and decided to go back home. The following December I went back to that rink knowing that I could now skate without falling down. The same tourist entered the rink thinking the same thing. I followed her around just in case, and sure enough she fell again. We were very excited to see each other again at this unexpected meeting one year later. The bartender looked at us as he placed our drinks on the bar before we could even order them. He circled the area in a counter clockwise direction, serving his drinks as my girl and I knew something special was about to take place. Before her trip back home, she accepted my proposal of marriage. It wasn't too long after that we felt the need for a slow dance at our wedding. There was no dizziness or being unbalanced as we felt the urge to go in a counter clockwise direction. On loves path sometimes we meet on skates where falling down has a need to be picked up once again. Whether it is from right to left or left to right, doesn't really matter....

That Will Last...

Between a dream and reality, there is me and you. A fine line of hugs and kisses that may be forgotten or remembered upon awakening or walking in and out of our front door. So how far do our pillows sit where maps and directions haven't a clue. Maybe half way we can meet if only for a moment that will last forever....

The Lifting Of Veil...

Perhaps this story will change the way people think about how love progresses, perhaps not. Without mentioning names, here is how it started...Two grade school kids bobbing up and down in a playground during recess on a seesaw. They held hands on their way back to class and pecked a kiss on each other's cheek before entering the door. It was something that would continue into high school and college and beyond as these two love birds never parted. He lifted her veil of the wedding outfit and kissed the bride as if it was for the first time. Both were the same age and this marriage took place when they were twenty five. A baby girl was born nine months later and the following year, a boy. Mom and dad sat on a seesaw in a playground one Sunday when school was closed. It was just for old times' sake where their first memory of holding hands and a first kiss had happened. Candlelit dinners on weekends after the kids were tucked in were a regular thing with them. They both retired from their jobs at the age where most do that. The kids had moved out and had children of their own but would still keep in touch and visit mom and dad when they could. At seventy two his wife passed from natural causes of heart failure. He lifted the veil surrounding her hospital bed and kissed her goodbye while holding her hand at the same time. One month later my soul told me that I could continue here no longer without her. My son and daughter along with my grandchildren lifted the veil that surrounded my hospital bed and kissed me goodbye. I found myself drifting towards a beautiful and loving white light. My twenty five year old bride was there waiting for me once again. On loves path we sit in playgrounds and graduate schools. Sometimes it happens to be the same one where holding hands and kissing continues on. It may be just my opinion, but what else can I say except for the lifting of veil....

Prologue

Thank you so much for reading my stories; it has been my pleasure to share them with you. If I have touched you or made you feel good in your own special way, then I have served a purpose. I will continue with writing my fourth book "A Matter Of Healing". If you have read my first two books "Incredible Short Stories" and "Where Angels Tread", then you know where I am coming from. It is you who I write to, just for spreading some good feelings which are needed in our world today and tomorrow. God bless, sleep tight, and pleasant dreams.

Love,
Michael Reisman

Printed in the United States
by Baker & Taylor Publisher Services